MW01128675

THE CAT COLLECTOR

Three Cozy Mystery Novellas

By
LORI HERTER

Copyright 2019 by Lori Herter

All rights reserved. No part of this book may be reproduced in any form or by any electronic or mechanical means including information storage and retrieval systems—except in the case of brief quotations in articles or reviews—without the permission in writing from its publisher, Lori Herter.

All brand names and product names used in this book are trademarks, registered trademarks, or trade names of their respective holders. I am not associated with any product or vendor in this book.

This is a work of fiction. All situations, characters and concepts are the sole invention of the author or are used fictitiously.

Published in the United States of America.

An earlier version of the opening novella in this volume, "The Coffee Caper," was previously published by Lori Herter under the title "A Murder Brewing" in an anthology titled "Murder, Mystery & Mayhem" compiled and published by Orange County Fictionaires in 2017.

ACKNOWLEDGEMENTS

Many thanks to Licensed Veterinary Technician Lisa Gregory for her expertise in veterinary work, and for reading my novellas to make sure my descriptions of pet clinic procedures are correct.

Cover design by Mariah Sinclair

www.mariahsinclair.com

TABLE OF CONTENTS

THE COFFEE CAPER

THE WINGED WITNESS

THE CLAIRVOYANT CAT

5

THE CAT COLLECTOR

Novella I
THE COFFEE CAPER

Chapter 1: A Clerical Error

Claudia Bailey did her best to tune out the noise level at the Bumblebee Café, bustling as usual at noontime. Located in a western suburb of Chicago, the historic eatery, built of brick with big windowpanes, faced the First Presbyterian Church across the street. Both buildings were vibrant remnants of the early 1900's. She glanced out the window at the white stucco church with its bell tower, beautifully set off by a few large oak trees in full autumn colors, and a green lawn. Quaint and picturesque, First Presbyterian made a popular wedding venue. Claudia and her husband had been married there. And eleven years later his funeral service had been held there.

Sitting in one of Bumblebee's vintage wooden booths, casually dressed in pants and a sweater, Claudia was feeling disheartened and confused. "Wish our sweet old Pastor Collins hadn't retired," she told her friend Amy Kopecky. "Glen McGrath is so different. He says one thing, does another. His sermons are simplistic. He and his wife seem contemptuous of our church's customs. Even the pancake breakfast!"

Their blue jean-clad young waitress brought the ice teas they ordered. Claudia and Amy had walked over to the restaurant for lunch after spending their Saturday morning setting up and decorating tables for the church's annual pancake breakfast in Fellowship Hall the next morning, a church tradition so old no one remembered anymore why it was held.

"I wonder if McGrath and his wife will even come," Amy said, pushing her medium-length curly red hair out of her face.

"What did the Pastor Nominating Committee see in him?" Claudia wondered aloud with puzzled annoyance. She glanced around the crowded restaurant, hoping no other church members had come in. Lowering her voice, she added, "Of the bunch of resumes they considered, McGrath's was the best they could find?"

"I think they made a clerical error," Amy darkly quipped, her hoop earrings dangling as she spoke. "Mostly due to Sue Ember's influence, from what I hear."

Claudia had to agree. "Sue was on the PNC. And she's had a high profile around church for a long time. Years. I used to like her well enough, even though she's so conservative, her dad having been a fundamentalist minister and all. But lately, she's gotten a little full of herself."

"And she's been wearing eye-makeup and lipstick. She always looked so plain. What's up with that?" Amy asked. "Hasn't she always said she met the love of her life in high school, but he died? Never met anyone she could love as much, and that's why she's a forty-something spinster. Is she having a mid-life crisis?"

"I have no idea," Claudia said. "I had a wonderful husband. When he passed away, I decided I'd never remarry. But the last year or two, I've begun to think if I met a nice guy, maybe I could fall in love again. I'm pushing forty. Is that a sign of a mid-life crisis?"

Amy perked up. "So you're looking to date?"

Claudia smiled and adjusted the tortoiseshell barrette that held back her long blond hair at the nape of her neck. "I'm open to the idea. Not desperately looking. No need for you and Larry to try to play matchmaker."

8

"Larry's got some single co-workers at his CPA firm . . . ."

"Never mind," Claudia said with an indulgent sigh. She knew Amy, like the good friend she was, only wanted Claudia to be happy. "Let's get back to McGrath. He's so hard to figure out. I don't know who he is. When the Adult Ed committee met two weeks ago, he sat there silently, like he couldn't make up his mind if he was annoyed or bored. I even caught him rolling his eyes. He's been here over six months. You'd think he'd be more in sync with us by now."

"The Adult Ed committee is probably way too progressive for him," Amy said. "Aren't you putting on that discussion program between a Christian minister, a Rabbi and an Imam?"

Claudia nodded. "A Trialogue. The retired minister who organizes it named it that. They're booked up months in advance. We finally were able to pencil them in on the church calendar for the second Saturday in January." She paused. "Now that I think of it, it's when we were discussing it that McGrath rolled his eyes."

"Well," Amy jested in a sarcastic tone, "he wouldn't want any non-Christian darkening our door. I bet he'd even frown on a Catholic priest."

Claudia shook her head with dismay. "Sadly, we're in an era where people are afraid of others who follow a different faith. A lot of members like Sue are quite drawn to McGrath. He's become more openly conservative than when he first came. Like

9

he has a hidden agenda. Feeding their fears. It's unsettling."

Amy leaned across the table. "Larry told me something even more unsettling. Keep this to yourself."

"Sure," Claudia said.

"Remember when McGrath was voted in? He signed a contract to receive a certain salary. Soon after, he talked to my husband and indignantly complained that the salary he'd agreed to wasn't enough for him to live on. He said the church owed him an adequate income. Larry was taken aback, but he chairs the Finance Committee and discussed it with them. They all have financial backgrounds and managed to find ways to legally dip into memorial funds and give McGrath the salary he wanted. He got a big raise, and he'd only just started."

Claudia leaned back, dumbfounded. "Why didn't they sue him for breach of contract or something?"

Amy shrugged. "McGrath was the PNC's choice, so they felt he should be given a chance. They met with him privately and went over his finances. Turned out he came to us already carrying a big credit card debt. So Larry asked him, 'Why did you agree to our offer if you knew it wouldn't be enough?' McGrath said he felt a sacred call to our church and trusted God would lead him and us in the way to resolve his money problems."

"So God was his co-conspirator in keeping his debt secret?" Claudia commented in a dry tone as she turned to glance around the restaurant again.

Amy spread her hands. "Unbelievable, isn't it? Larry has tried to give him some financial counseling, but McGrath seems to resent being schooled about his personal—"

"We better cool it," Claudia interrupted. "Sue Ember just walked in."

Amy turned to look. "Oh, no. Do we have to invite her to sit with us?"

Claudia sighed. "I'm afraid so. She's my neighbor—lives a block away. And she brings her cat to the clinic. Our office manager wouldn't like me alienating a client." Claudia worked as a veterinary technician at the Briarwood Cat Clinic.

Hiding her reluctance, Claudia smiled as she waved at Sue and motioned her to come to their table.

Her tall, full figure covered by a loose chambray tunic over black polyester pants, Sue looked awkward as she walked up to their table. "Hi," she said, sounding a trifle uneasy as she smoothed her thick brunette hair, cut in a precise Dutch boy style. Her dark eyebrows were curiously uneven, with one brow arched higher than the other, matching the slightly unbalanced contours of her face. "Could've figured I'd find you here. I just finished putting the flowers on the tables in Fellowship Hall."

11

"You did a nice job," Amy said affably. "I saw you in the church kitchen arranging all those vases."

"Thank you." Sue took an arch tone. "Even Jo Louise McGrath managed to compliment me on them."

"The pastor's wife stopped by?" Claudia said with surprise. "Come and sit with us. We ordered sandwiches, but they aren't here yet."

"Oh, she stopped by—for five whole minutes," Sue said with a sniff as she sat down in the booth next to Amy, who obligingly moved over. "Jo Louise—what a snooty name, huh? Those hawkish eyes. She's been getting more involved, trying to bring our activities up to her standards. She's only three feet tall, but she still manages to look down her nose at everybody."

Claudia and Amy laughed.

"I think she's at least five foot two," Claudia said. "Sounds like you don't cotton to her."

"Do you like her?" Sue countered.

Claudia tilted her head. "Not exactly, but she does seem to try to be the perfect pastor's wife."

"OMG, it's like she's from central casting!" Sue exclaimed. "She's got him wrapped around her perfectly polished little finger."

"Tell us how you really feel," Amy joked, her green eyes sparkling.

"I will! He has to take her out to dinner at The Old Mill every week. You know what an overpriced restaurant that is. Probably so she can show off the expensive clothes she buys."

12

"I've heard he has financial problems," Amy ventured. "Jo Louise does have a nice wardrobe. You think his wife's a spendthrift?"

"I'm sure of it," Sue declared.

"But you still like Reverend McGrath, right?" Claudia asked, trying to understand Sue's point of view. "You always speak up for him if he gets criticized."

"Oh, absolutely," Sue said. "He's the best thing that ever happened to our church. The Lord is definitely working through him. He'll get us on the right path."

"I didn't know our church was on the wrong path," Amy muttered.

"It's just too bad he was dazzled by a pretty face," Sue went on, "and married someone who only thinks of herself."

"But you just said it's like she's from central casting. The perfect minister's wife," Claudia reminded her.

"Yeah, but it's all an act," Sue insisted. "All her gracious empathy. She's a big phony. She's said some pretty snippy things to me. A real two-face."

The waitress came by with the sandwiches Claudia and Amy had ordered. "Sorry, it took so long," she said as she set the plates on the table. "We're pretty busy." She looked at Sue. "What can I get you? Ice tea? Coffee?"

Sue made a face. "Ugh, I hate coffee. Diet cola and a tuna on rye, please."

"Coming right up." The waitress hurried off.

Amy chewed a French fry, her eyes crinkling impishly as she glanced at the woman next to her. "Speaking of coffee, Sue, my husband says that our Reverend McGrath bought a pricey new espresso machine for his office, along with a posh Aubusson rug. And he used the Wedding Committee's money to pay for them. The ladies on that committee need to buy a new white carpet for the center aisle, and discovered their budget was depleted. You know anything about that? Did Jo Louise insist he buy those items?"

Sue squared her shoulders and her expression toughened. "No. He wants to have a cozy environment when he counsels couples about to be married. He's thoughtful about things like that."

"But he didn't get church approval," Amy said. "The Finance Committee didn't know about it anymore than the Wedding Committee."

"He's our pastor," Sue declared indignantly. "Our shepherd sent by the Lord. Why should he have to get approval?"

"Because that's the way the Presbyterian Church does things," Amy argued. "He's not following rules."

Oh, boy. Claudia nervously scratched her nose. *Change the subject.* "You have a new haircut, Sue. Looks great."

Sue seemed disconcerted by the sudden shift, but her stern brown eyes softened as she seemed to take Claudia's hint. "Thanks," she said. "Got a new hairdresser. She showed me how to do make-up, too."

"I've noticed," Claudia said. "You look very nice. More polished and sophisticated. Looks like you've lost some weight, too."

Sue smiled with pride. "Thirteen pounds. Working to whittle off more. When I was young, I was a size ten. Aiming for that again."

Apparently following Claudia's lead, Amy took on a friendly tone. "While I'm thinking of it, Sue, I have a crystal pitcher to donate for the Silent Auction. You're collecting items for that, aren't you? When is it?"

"The Silent Auction is set for the second Saturday in January. I'll start taking items after New Year's."

Claudia looked up from eating her turkey sandwich with alarm. "That can't be right. The Trialogue is set for that evening. I watched Verna put it on the church calendar myself, months ago." Verna was the church's longtime secretary.

"That date was empty when I saw the calendar," Sue said blithely. "I penciled in the Silent Auction myself."

"But . . . how can that be?" Claudia said, aghast. "How could what Verna wrote have disappeared?"

"Beats me," Sue said.

"On Monday, go to the church office and ask Verna. She'll know," Amy told Claudia.

"You bet I will!"

Sue chuckled. "Good luck."

Claudia wanted to ask Sue what she meant by her snarky "good luck," but the waitress arrived with Sue's cola and sandwich. The disruption caused Claudia to think better of starting another conversational minefield.

Instead she asked Sue, "How's your cat?"

"Knickerbocker's been okay. Peeing in the litter pan more than usual though. Maybe because he's getting old?"

As Claudia came up with reasons why a cat might pee more, she noticed Amy looking up at the ceiling, obviously stifling her impatience. She felt bad that Amy was getting irritated, all because Claudia felt she had to invite Sue to join them. But by this point, Claudia knew discussing a cat's litter pan habits was a lot safer than church talk.

Chapter 2: Amaretto Ambrosia

On Monday, Claudia left the cat clinic to take her lunch break. She drove to the church, parked, and walked into the office to the left of the sanctuary. The office was not large, with a reception desk, a small conference room, another room that contained the Xerox machine and other equipment, and four small offices, the largest one belonging to the pastor.

Destiny Gorski, the twenty-year-old receptionist who sported a fuchsia streak in her short black hair, looked up and smiled. "Hi Claudia. How are you?"

"Fine, thanks. Is Verna here?"

"Verna's at lunch." Destiny blinked her thickly mascaraed lashes. "Can I help?"

Disappointed, Claudia asked, "May I have a look at the big calendar? I thought I had a Saturday reserved for the Trialogue."

"Sure, let's go look." Destiny tugged down her tight mini-skirt as she rose from her seat behind the counter.

They walked into the conference room, where on a small desk in one corner the official church calendar was kept. Destiny paged through it to the date Claudia gave her. They both peered at the lines allotted to the second Saturday in January.

"It says, 'Silent Auction.'" Destiny glanced at Claudia. "It does look like something was erased underneath."

At that moment, the pastor's door opened, bringing forth a whiff of coffee. Claudia straightened her back when she saw Glen McGrath stroll out. Middling tall, thinning brown hair, forty-something, with a face that was neither homely nor handsome, he was curiously non-descript. He glanced at Claudia, his face blandly impenetrable.

"Going to lunch," he told Destiny. "Hello, Claudia." He barely nodded.

The phone rang and Destiny hurried back to her desk.

"Can I ask you something?" Claudia said. "Verna put the Trialogue on the calendar months ago. But now it shows the Silent Auction on that night."

"Really." His tone sounded like puzzled interest. "Well, Verna is getting on in years." His brows drew together in a concerned expression. "She's been fuzzy-headed, getting things mixed up. It doesn't surprise me that she changed something in her confusion."

Claudia stared at him. "Verna, fuzzy-headed?" Verna was white-haired and past seventy, but she seemed as sharp as she ever was.

"Oh, yes," McGrath said with a sharp exhale. "I'm having a difficult time with her. Sad, but I think it's time she retired. My wife would be a great secretary. I'm going to talk to the Personnel Committee about it."

Claudia merely nodded as she stifled her anger. "So . . . what about the Trialogue? Do I call the pastor who runs it and say we have to change the date?"

McGrath's expression grew opaque again. "Tell him we've decided our church is not a suitable venue for that kind of event."

"How is it not suitable?"

"We're all about leading people to know and follow our Lord Jesus Christ. A Jew and a Muslim wouldn't feel comfortable here. They have their places of worship."

"But it's meant to be a friendly discussion so we can learn more about each other."

"We have the Lord," he said sternly, chin in the air as if he towered over her, though he didn't. "We don't need to hear ideas that might lead us astray."

Claudia lowered her eyes and took a step back. "I see." Her voice tightened. "But our church already approved it."

"I'm sure your Interim Pastor tried to keep everyone happy during the transition from the long years under your former minister. But I intend to make First Presbyterian a strictly faith-based church."

McGrath walked past her and left. Claudia took a deep breath, infuriated and disconcerted. The door to McGrath's office was left open and she still smelled coffee. Claudia stepped to the door and noticed a side table on which stood a fancy, shiny coffee maker. Not the usual Keurig, but one that made gourmet coffee drinks. Beside it was a box of pods for the machine. She also saw the plush Aubusson throw rug on the floor, just as Amy had said.

She went out to the reception desk. Destiny was no longer on the phone.

"I see he has an espresso machine."

Destiny nodded with a huffy sigh. "He loves his lattes. I have to keep it filled with water and buy the right flavor of little pods. Has to be Amaretto Ambrosia or he's in a snit. If the store's out of it, he blames me for not stocking up."

"Sounds like he's not much fun to work with," Claudia said.

"I loved my job when Pastor Collins was here. He always told us to call him John. McGrath insists we call him *Reverend* McGrath. Makes snide jokes about the streak in my hair and how I dress. Oh and he said I should change my name. He goes, 'Destiny sounds like a singer in a sleazy rock band.' I just snapped. I go, 'Cool! I'm wild about rock bands!' Boy did he give me an ugly look. Said any more back talk and he can have me fired."

"How awful," Claudia said in disbelief.

"I think he's hoping I'll quit so he can replace me. Maybe with Sue Ember, who's here an awful lot lately. Sue's taking over for Mattie while she's recovering from heart surgery. But Mattie only needed to come in once a week to do the

20

bookkeeping. Sometimes I wonder if Sue is cooking the church books, she's here so much."

"I hope McGrath doesn't harass you into quitting," Claudia said, deeply troubled by what she was hearing.

"With my brother in rehab and my mom needing hip replacement, I have enough stress without worrying if I have to find a new job."

"How is your brother?"

Destiny made a tentative smile. "He's off drugs for three weeks now, so Mom and I are hopeful. But Mom's worn to the bone worrying."

"McGrath should be supporting you, not threatening you. Hang in there," Claudia said in a reassuring way. "We're all praying for your family." She turned to leave, but was happy to see Verna walk in, her thin figure neatly dressed in pants and a flowered jacket.

"Just the person I wanted to see," Claudia said to the frail lady with curly white hair and blue-framed bifocals that matched her pale blue eyes. "I'm wondering why the Trialogue was removed from the calendar."

Verna's head went back. "It was?" She headed for the conference room, followed by Claudia and Destiny.

"Oh, for heaven's sake." Verna shook her head as she looked at the evidence. "I didn't change it." She glanced at Destiny. "I'm sure you didn't either."

Destiny also shook her head. "That leaves two possibilities. McGrath or Sue Ember."

"Sue would do something like that?" Claudia said with surprise.

"Oh, she covers up for him a lot," Destiny replied. "The other day I happened to catch her when she was marking his receipts from The Old Mill. He takes his wife there, but I peeked over Sue's shoulder and could see she was noting each one as a church expense, like he was counselling people over dinner."

"Isn't he supposed to do that in his office?" Claudia said.

"Of course," Verna agreed. "But this way he can sneak his wife to a fancy restaurant at the church's expense." Verna's gaze intensified as she looked at Claudia. "He wants her to take over my job. When I told him I need to work three more years to have enough money to retire on, he said, 'You're a tool of the devil!'"

"What?!" Claudia exclaimed.

"I heard him say that to her," Destiny affirmed.

"I'm in his way, you see," Verna said, "so I'm from the devil. With me gone, his wife could earn my salary. He claims that's God's plan."

"He knows Verna and I are on to him," Destiny said. "So he hassles us, hoping we'll quit."

Verna turned to Destiny. "If you leave, what would I do? I don't know if I can cope here on my own. But I need to work, and who else would hire a seventy-two year old woman?" Tears filled her eyes.

Destiny slipped her arm around Verna's shoulders. "Don't you worry. We'll tough it out together." She looked at Claudia. "Unless he can find some legal way to fire us, we're staying."

"Good for you." Claudia blinked back tears for their plight. "You should talk to the Personnel Committee. This sort of harassment ought to be reported to the Chicago Presbytery," she said, referring to the ruling body of the local Presbyterian churches.

"Oh, I'd be afraid to," Verna said, wiping her eyes. "I don't know what he'd do if he found out. Come to my house and murder me!"

"Is he violent?" Claudia asked with alarm.

"He has a bad temper," Destiny said. "Last week he threw a book at the wall when I'd run out of his stupid Amaretto Ambrosia."

Burdened by all she'd heard, Claudia expressed her support and said goodbye. She had to get back to work.

At the Briarwood Cat Clinic a few hours later, she learned Sue had brought in her Maine Coon cat.

Mary Anne Portnoy, the clinic's young, ponytailed receptionist had taken Sue and her pet into one of the two examination rooms, painted in soft tones of beige and green. A poster of three cats in the Coliseum in Rome hung on one wall.

Claudia put on a smile as she entered. "So you decided to bring Knickerbocker in?"

"He's still peeing too much," Sue said, petting the cat's thick grey-brown fur. Knickerbocker nestled against her as she worked to keep the cat on the stainless steel exam table.

"Well, it could be a UTI. But he's an older cat, so his kidneys may be showing his age," Claudia said as she took the cat's temperature, inserting a thermometer under his tail while Sue helped to keep him still.

Claudia checked the thermometer. "He has a bit of a fever," she said, making a note for the veterinarian. After also taking notes on Knickerbocker's pulse and respiration, she said, "Dr. Chandler will be in to examine him. I'm anticipating he'll want me to take a urine sample."

"Does that hurt?" Sue's eyes sharpened with concern.

"Not usually. The cat doesn't know it's going to be stuck with a needle." Claudia swallowed and decided to ask the question on her mind. "By the way, I stopped at church, and you were right about the Silent Auction. Do you have any idea who erased the Trialogue off the calendar?"

Sue shrugged. "I didn't. Maybe it was Verna. Glen says she's getting senile."

Glen? Claudia hid her surprise at Sue's first name basis with the pastor. "I don't think Verna is one bit senile. I suspect Reverend McGrath made the change."

"Well, if he did," Sue said in a regal manner, "he had a good reason."

24

Dr. August Chandler, a grandfatherly, white-haired veterinarian, came in then and Claudia left. As she'd predicted, about ten minutes later, Dr. Chandler brought Knickerbocker into the treatment room and Claudia used a syringe to withdraw some of the cat's urine to be analyzed. She managed to keep the beautiful, emerald-eyed Maine Coon calm. He seemed to trust her and barely noticed when she inserted the syringe. Claudia carried the big feline back to Sue, who was waiting in the exam room.

"He was a good kitty. Got an adequate sample," she told Sue, who looked relieved. "If there is bacteria, then we'll need to send it out to be cultured, so Dr. Chandler can prescribe the appropriate antibiotic."

"I'll have to give him a medication?" Sue's expression grew apprehensive. "Hope it's a liquid," she said, cuddling the fluffy cat purring in her arms. "I've never been able to get a pill down his throat."

"We'll cross that bridge if we come to it," Claudia said.

As she drove home from work that evening, Claudia mulled over what she'd learned from Verna, Destiny, and also Sue. When she got home, she phoned Amy and asked if they could meet for lunch the next day.

Chapter 3: Holy Hell

"Working at the church must be holy hell," Claudia quipped after filling Amy in on her visit the day before. They were sitting in a corner booth at a modern, colorfully painted café called Super Soups, located within walking distance of the cat clinic.

"Sounds horrible," Amy agreed. "Glad I can be a stay-at-home mom."

Claudia stirred her still steaming bowl of chicken and rice soup. "I wonder how Sue has so much time to volunteer at the church? Doesn't she work as a bookkeeper at an electronics factory?"

Amy's green eyes brightened. "Larry and I happened to sit in front of Sue on Sunday. I overheard her telling the lady next to her that she's gone to part time at her job because, as she put it, 'the church needs me.' She said she inherited money from an aunt, so she's okay financially to stay in the bungalow she rents for the next few years."

"Hmm." Claudia squinted at her friend. "And you just 'happened' to sit in the pew in front of her?"

"Okay, so I'm nosey. That pew was half empty, so I told Larry let's sit there. Sue's kind of an oddball. I'm still curious if she's in a mid-life crisis or if she's got a man in her life. Which reminds me, are you dating anyone yet?"

Claudia sighed with a smile. "No. I'm in no hurry."

"You'll get nowhere with that attitude."

"Amy, if God wants me to meet someone, the right guy will cross my path. Meanwhile, I enjoy my job, I'm used to living alone, and I'm happy as is."

"If you say so." Amy swallowed a spoonful of her kale and bean soup. "So what are you going to do about the Trialogue?"

Claudia shook her head, keeping a lid on her anger so as not to raise her voice in the restaurant. "It makes me so mad whenever I think about McGrath's underhandedness. I'm going to ask him point blank if he's the one who erased it. Shouldn't people confront him when he lies?"

"I think so. Otherwise he'll keep getting away with it." Amy grinned. "You go girl!"

#

The next morning, after spending the prior evening practicing what she'd say to McGrath, Claudia left the cat clinic at nine a.m. and drove to the church office. It was Wednesday, the day the clinic opened up at seven a.m. to accommodate clients whose schedules required them to bring in their pet early. After working two hours, Claudia had asked for time off to run a personal errand.

She noticed McGrath's red Cadillac Escalade in the church parking lot as she got out of her Prius. When she entered the office she saw Destiny and Verna at their desks.

27

"Is he in?" she asked Destiny.

"Must be. Haven't seen him. Probably working on his sermon."

Claudia walked to the pastor's door and knocked. There was no answer, but the door came open a bit. She smelled a faint whiff of coffee and knocked again. When there was still no answer, she slowly pushed on the door. "Hello?"

She peeked in and saw McGrath in a striped shirt and pants lying face down on the Aubusson carpet. A spilled mug of dark liquid lay on its side next to his hand, the wet stain soaking into the thick aqua and ivory fibers.

Claudia gasped and walked up to him, bending to tap his shoulder. She noticed a peculiar odor. "Are you okay?" He did not move. "Destiny! Verna! Call 911!"

In about five minutes sirens blared outside the church as the three women waited in a quiet panic. Claudia hurried to direct the ambulance crew to the office. She and Destiny waited outside McGrath's partly open door as the paramedics tried to revive him. Verna sat at her desk in white-faced shock.

Soon more sirens blared outside, startling the women. Three policemen and a policewoman dressed in blue uniforms walked in. The church office began to feel crowded.

"Who found the body?" one of them asked.

"I did," Claudia said with a gulp. *The body? Was he dead?*

"Work here?" he asked.

28

"No, just a church member." She introduced him to Destiny and Verna.

The stout young cop instructed them to stay nearby. "Detective O'Rourke is on his way. He'll want to ask some questions."

Claudia looked at the other two women, their faces reflecting the same apprehension she was feeling. "What's going on?" she mouthed to them. Then she realized she needed to alert the clinic that she'd be delayed.

She was on her cell phone with Trudy, the clinic's manager, when a tall man with graying brown hair, looking fit and forty-five or so, walked in wearing a dark blue suit and striped tie. Figuring this was the detective, she ended the call.

Claudia saw his sharp gaze shift from her and Destiny to Verna, still looking pale at her desk. He pulled out his badge. "Detective Steve O'Rourke. Briarwood Police." His brown eyes settled on Claudia. "Were you here when the body was discovered?"

"I opened the door to talk to him and there he was on the floor," Claudia told him, her voice sounding breathless.

"Please wait outside." After glancing at Verna, he asked one of the paramedics who was packing up his equipment to check on her. He walked into McGrath's office and closed the door. One of the uniformed policemen escorted Claudia and Destiny into the courtyard, where the women sat down on one of the benches while the police officer stood nearby. Soon a photographer arrived. Another uniformed officer began placing yellow crime scene tape across the church office's entrance.

Taking all this in, Claudia asked the stoic-faced young policeman standing near them, "Was McGrath murdered?" She remembered the odor she'd noticed when she found him. It might have been bitter almond which, according to murder mysteries she'd read, was what cyanide smelled like.

"They're investigating his death," was all the officer would say.

In a while, O'Rourke lithely ducked under the yellow tape stretched across the door and approached Claudia and Destiny.

"The paramedics are giving the lady inside oxygen. Is there someplace I can interview you?" he asked.

"Fellowship Hall," Destiny said.

He followed them the twenty yards to the double doors of a rectangular brick building. Destiny found her keys and unlocked it.

Claudia assumed they all would go in, but he surprised her by asking Destiny to wait on the bench again under the uniformed officer's watchful eye.

"Come with me, please," he said to Claudia, who wondered if she was a suspect because she'd found McGrath.

A long table and folding chairs had been set up for a committee meeting in one corner of the large, linoleum-tiled hall. He asked her to sit down and he took a seat across from her. He pulled out a notepad and then a digital recorder and set them on the table between them, causing Claudia to draw in a deep, uneasy breath. She'd never been under the scrutiny of a police detective before. Or been part of a crime scene.

"Just routine." He asked for her full name and wrote it down. He turned on the recorder and stated the time and place, and who was present. Then he looked up at her. "You said you came to talk to the pastor? What time did you get here?"

"About nine-fifteen," she replied, being as accurate as she could. "The church office opens at nine. I saw his red car."

O'Rourke nodded. "What did you want to talk to him about?"

She had to pull her thoughts together, rubbing her forehead with a shaking hand. "I knew he'd erased a program on the church calendar without telling anyone, blaming it on his secretary. He's been threatening her job, and Destiny's, too. Verna said she didn't erase it, and I believed her. I wanted to confront him about his lie."

"Is Verna the woman getting oxygen?"

"Yes. And Destiny's the receptionist waiting outside."

O'Rourke made a note. "Who else works in the church office, or has access?"

"Mattie's the bookkeeper, but she's recovering from heart surgery. Sue Ember, a church member, has been filling in for her."

The detective wrote on his pad, asking Claudia to spell everyone's full name. He looked up and raised one eyebrow. "Did you like McGrath?"

Claudia chewed her lip for a moment, wondering how much she should say. Sometimes she was too honest for her own good. But she knew being truthful was always best when dealing with the police. And he might find her input helpful.

"No. He was misusing church funds and lying to people. He's been here six months, and some of us think he came with a hidden agenda. He was extremely conservative." She explained how he'd put the kibosh on the Trialogue. "But he has . . . did have loyal followers like Sue Ember. They thought he was wonderful."

O'Rourke looked at her directly, his brown eyes unblinking. "Where were you before you came here to talk to him? Home?"

"At work. The clinic opens at seven on Wednesday."

"Clinic?"

"The Briarwood Cat Clinic on Main Street. I'm a licensed veterinary technician."

He eyed her clothes. "That's why you're wearing this outfit with cartoon cats, I suppose."

Claudia looked down at the tunic top she wore over white pants, one of several cheerfully printed scrubs she owned. Her face felt a bit warm as she

32

figured this no-nonsense police detective probably thought it looked childish.

"Were you alone at the clinic?" he asked.

"No, everyone was there. The veterinarian, the receptionist, the groomer and the woman who runs the office."

"So they can vouch for your whereabouts."

Claudia straightened her back against the metal chair. "You mean, do I have an alibi?" She felt affronted. "Yes, everyone saw me at work this morning." She paused. "I don't know what time McGrath died. I live alone and no one can attest that I was at home before I left for work."

"His body is still warm," O'Rourke said. "Probably dead less than an hour. But I have to ask these questions."

She bowed her head and nodded that she understood, nevertheless feeling horrified that he had thought she might be capable of murder.

"You have any reason to think McGrath might have killed himself?"

Claudia blinked at the idea. "He was too much of a narcissist." Her tone grew a bit sarcastic. "Besides, suicide is a sin and he wouldn't have wanted to meet his Maker that way." Immediately she wondered if she should have blurted that out.

O'Rourke smiled slightly as he wrote something more on his notepad. "I'll need your address and phone. May have further questions for you."

She gave him her information. As he wrote it down, he said without looking up, "You live alone. You're single?"

"A widow. My husband died several years ago."

He folded up his notepad and turned off the digital recorder. "Thank you. You can go now." He pulled a card out of his suit jacket. "Call me if you think of anything that might be pertinent," he said, looking up as he gave it to her.

Claudia's hand was still shaking as she took the card. She felt a little strange and lost as she met his steady gaze.

O'Rourke's eyes softened. "Finding a dead body is a shock. But you seem like a strong person." He rose from his chair. "You'll be okay," he added, reassurance in his voice.

They walked out together. Destiny was still sitting in the courtyard and he called her in to be interviewed next.

Feeling numb, Claudia was anxious to get back to the clinic and her normal life. But she wanted to check on Verna. She was relieved to see Verna standing outside the church office, thanking the paramedics who were leaving. Verna's color was good and she seemed to have recovered.

"Are you alright?" Claudia asked, walking up to her.

"I'm fine. Nice to have handsome young men fussing over me," she said. "I suppose that detective will want to interview me, too. What a morning! Who would have thought this would happen?"

"What a morning," Claudia agreed. "At least you won't have to worry about your job anymore." As she walked to her car, Claudia wondered if saving her job could have been motivation enough for Verna . . . .

How can you even think such a thing? Claudia got in her Prius and slammed the door.

Verna was no murderer. Nor was Destiny, even though she despised McGrath. Claudia hoped Detective O'Rourke wouldn't suspect them if they couldn't vouch for their whereabouts. Verna lived by herself. Destiny lived with her mother, but often joked how she sometimes stayed out all night with friends. They both had keys to the church. And access to McGrath's coffee maker, if his cup of coffee really was what killed him.

But Claudia could never believe anyone connected with the church who disliked McGrath would ever think of murdering him. Which left the question, who did kill him? *Was* it suicide?

Before going in to work, Claudia sat in her car in the cat clinic's parking lot and called Amy on her cell phone.

"You're joking, right?" Amy chuckled at what Claudia told her.

"No. McGrath was sprawled out on the fancy rug, next to a coffee spill. The paramedics called the police. I wonder if his coffee was poisoned."

"He's really dead?" Amy exclaimed.

35

"The detective asked if I thought McGrath might have killed himself, but I said I didn't think so."

"No," Amy agreed. "Was he murdered?"

"I don't know, but the detective asked me if I had an alibi! Fortunately my coworkers saw me at work at seven."

"Wow," Amy said. "What a lovely day you're having. I won't miss McGrath, but people at church will be upset whether they liked him or not. I wonder who could have killed him?"

"Can't imagine. I'm afraid this detective might suspect Verna or Destiny," Claudia said.

"What's the detective like?"

"Sort of a just-the-facts guy. Polite. At the end he tried to reassure me."

"How old?"

"Oh, maybe a few years older than me. Graying a little. Kind of nice looking."

"What's his name?"

"Steve O'Rourke."

"Irish, like you," Amy said.

"So was McGrath," Claudia reminded her.

Amy didn't seem to hear. "Did he wear a wedding ring?"

Claudia had to laugh. "Never occurred to me to look. Bye, Amy. Have to get back to work."

She was glad Amy had made her chuckle. It helped release the nervous energy still coursing through her.

Late in the morning the results for Sue's cat came in positive for a urinary tract infection, so Claudia had the sample sent to a lab to be cultured. She called Sue to tell her.

"The culture takes a few days, and then Dr. Chandler will give you the right medication."

"Hope it's not a pill," Sue said, sounding distressed. "Poor Knickerbocker."

"You live so close to me, I can always stop by your house and give him the pill."

"Oh, that's a relief," Sue said. "Thanks a mil, Claudia."

"No problem." Claudia hesitated. "So . . . did you hear about Reverend McGrath?"

"What about him?" Sue replied.

"He was found dead in his office this morning."

"He was?" Sue's breathing sounded uneven. "Oh, no. It can't be true."

"Sorry to be the bearer of bad news. I know you thought highly of him."

"Yes, I did," Sue said, her voice breaking. "I . . . I need to hang up. I'm so shocked."

"I understand. I'll phone when Knickerbocker's medication is ready." As she ended the call, Claudia felt some empathy for Sue, knowing McGrath's blind-faith followers would certainly miss him. She wondered if their church could recover from such a trauma.

Chapter 4: Losing Objectivity

The next day, Thursday, Claudia was assisting Dr. Chandler as he extracted a cat's bad tooth, when Mary Anne, the receptionist, hurried in.

"Sorry to interrupt, but there's a detective here." Her wide blue eyes fixed on Claudia. "He's asking about you. I slipped away to tell you."

Dr. Chandler looked up from the anesthetized cat. "I'm almost finished," he told Claudia. "You can go."

Worried, Claudia took off her face mask and latex exam gloves before going out to the front office. There she saw Detective Steve O'Rourke talking to Trudy Avery, the clinic's manager, a middle-aged blonde.

"Thanks," he was saying. "Just had to verify she was here from seven to nine, that's all."

He had to check my alibi? Claudia stepped up to him, wondering why he was still suspicious of her. "Satisfied?"

He seemed slightly taken aback. "Somewhere we can talk? I have more questions."

"The second exam room," Trudy said. "We put Sassafras in there for a little exercise, but you can talk there."

"This way." Claudia felt unsettled as she led him into the exam room. "Careful of the cat," she said, opening the glass door. She stooped to pick up Sassafras, a fluffy calico Persian, before the cat

38

could scoot out, then closed the door after the detective. She put Sassafras back on the floor. "She's being boarded while her family is on vacation. We let her in here when we can so she's not confined all the time."

"Okay," O'Rourke said matter-of-factly, though he looked a little mystified. "I'm not used to cats. Had a dog once, but . . . ."

"Your dog died?" she said, motioning him to sit on the built-in bench near the exam table. She pulled out a three-legged stool from beneath the computer shelf and sat down.

He nodded, his expression somber. "In a bad car accident years ago. My wife was driving. She died, too."

"How awful," Claudia replied, stunned. "I'm so sorry. It's a terrible loss, isn't it? My husband died of leukemia."

"You told me you were a widow. You have kids?"

"No. We wanted to, but . . . ." She shrugged.

"I have a son. Away at college, studying law." He drew in a breath. "So then, down to business. In our investigation of McGrath's death, we found that one of the used pods collected from inside the coffee machine had evidence of cyanide. Question is, how did the pod get tampered with? There were no fingerprints on it. We figure someone wearing gloves may have used a syringe to inject the cyanide into the top of the pod. That hole got obliterated when the machine's plunger went into it to brew the coffee."

"So it *was* murder?" Claudia sighed with dismay.

"Well, if he was going to kill himself, why go to all that trouble? Cyanide isn't a painless way to die, and even if he didn't care about that, he could have just mixed it into his cup. Why hide the poison in a coffee pod? Also, no suicide note. His wife told me he had big plans. Wanted to use your church as a stepping stone to a mega church, maybe even be a televangelist."

"He didn't have the charisma," Claudia said, puzzled that McGrath could have had such aspirations.

"So," O'Rourke went on, "the reason I needed to verify your whereabouts was because I knew you have access to needles here. You give animals shots, don't you?"

Claudia's mouth dropped open. "I do. I'm a suspect?"

"Your co-workers affirmed you were here when he must have ingested the cyanide. I found I was losing my objectivity, so I went back to the basic police work of officially confirming what you told me. Though we don't know when the pod was tampered with. It might have been planted in McGrath's box of coffee. But then the perpetrator wouldn't know if McGrath would select that particular pod, or even offer coffee to someone else.

I'm going on the theory that the murderer made his coffee for him."

She wondered what the detective meant by losing his objectivity, but just then Sassafras jumped up onto the exam table between them. In the next moment, the cat pounced onto O'Rourke's lap. The detective's eyes widened in astonishment.

Claudia rose from her seat. "So sorry. I'll take her—"

"That's okay." He tentatively petted the cat's head.

"You'll have cat fur all over your suit," Claudia warned.

"There are worse things," he said. "She's purring."

Claudia grinned. "That's a compliment. Cats don't take to just anyone."

He chuckled. "I'm flattered." Pulling out his notebook and a pen from his jacket as the cat loudly purred, he said, "Whom do you know at the church who might have access to syringes? And cyanide."

Sitting down again, Claudia lifted her shoulders. "I have no idea where anyone would get cyanide. As for needles, well . . . ."

"What about Verna or Destiny?"

She was about to say no, but then she remembered. "Destiny's brother is in rehab for heroin addiction. I suppose there could still be needles at their home."

O'Rourke made a note. "Verna?"

"No," Claudia said.

"She have diabetes maybe?"

"Not that I know of. She's pretty healthy for seventy-two. Although," Claudia added with a sigh, "she has a cat that has failing kidneys. Dr. Chandler has her give the cat subcutaneous fluids. It's not done with a syringe, but a thicker type of needle that is attached to a bag of fluids and injected into the scruff of the neck. Maybe that could be rigged up somehow to inject something into a coffee pod. But Verna couldn't murder anyone. Neither could Destiny."

He lifted an ominous eyebrow. "People have killed for less than their job being threatened. Anyone else you can think of who might have a motive?"

Claudia bit her lip as she pictured names and faces. "No. He had followers like Sue who thought he was on God's holy wavelength. They even thought he had a sense of humor, and that he was good at making hospital and home visits. None of them wanted him dead."

"Sue Ember?" O'Rourke nodded. "I interviewed her. A true believer alright."

"There are others like me," Claudia went on, "who didn't like him and thought he'd wind up splitting the church. But there are legal ways in the Presbyterian hierarchy to get a minister booted out. No need to murder him."

"Okay. Thanks, Claudia." He folded up his notebook. "Can you provide me with one of those needles used to administer fluids?"

She rose. "Sure. I'd better take Sassafras back. They'll be needing this room soon." He looked up as she bent over him to lift the cat off his lap. Their eyes met and she was aware of his quiet but penetrating gaze, as though he wanted to know everything about her. Not as a detective, but as a man. Her heartbeat jumped into a new rhythm. She began to understand what he'd meant about losing his objectivity.

Claudia broke the eye contact by looking down at Sassafras as she picked up the feline. "Meet you out front, okay?"

In a few minutes, she handed him the needle he'd asked for as he stood in the waiting room.

"Thanks," he said. "Need it back?"

"No."

"I'll keep in touch," he told her, back to his matter-of-fact demeanor. "If you think of anything that might be useful, call me. Still have my card?"

She smiled. "Yes, I do, Steve."

His eyes brightened to a soft glow as she called him by his first name. And then he left.

Chapter 5: The Bride's Room

On Saturday afternoon, McGrath's funeral was held at the church. His closed casket was at the front. A minister had been sent from the Chicago Presbytery to preside. Claudia walked into the church sanctuary and sat next to Amy and Larry.

"Jo Louise looks all glamorous in her black suit and wide-brimmed black hat with that long feather," Amy commented, surreptitiously pointing to the minister's wife in the front pew. "As Sue said, it's like she's from central casting."

They watched Jo Louise greet some people who walked up to her. Claudia commented, "She does look stricken and tearful. Her eyes are red."

"She looks angry, too, don't you think?" Amy said.

Claudia pondered the slim, petite woman's expression. "You may be right. She's grieving, but brimming with pent up energy. Have you seen Sue?"

"Not so far. Verna and Destiny are over there toward the back."

The pews were filling up fast, Claudia noticed, turning to look around.

"Oh, Steve O'Rourke just came in," Claudia whispered to Amy with surprise. "Keeping his eye out for suspects?"

"Where?" Amy said with great interest.

"He's standing at the back of the far side aisle. Tall, blue suit."

Amy turned in a low-key manner to look. "That's your detective?" She shifted her keen gaze to Claudia. "He's hot!"

"He's not *my* detective," Claudia said, knowing Amy might already be visualizing a wedding. "He's investigating the case."

Amy looked over her shoulder again. "No ring on his left hand."

"His wife died in a car accident. He has a grown son."

"He's widowed, just like you," Amy said with eager interest.

"Yes, well, that's not exactly something to celebrate," Claudia quietly stated.

"Oh, sorry, I didn't mean—"

"I know." Claudia began to feel antsy. "I drank too much iced tea at lunch. Better hit the ladies' room."

Amy checked her watch. "Ten minutes before the service starts. Why don't you use the little bathroom in the bride's room? It's closer. Ladies' room might be full."

"Good idea."

Claudia found her way to the bride's room which was rather hidden at one side of the front of the sanctuary. Not everyone knew about it. She entered the small, carpeted room, sweetly decorated with flowered wallpaper, a velvet loveseat and a long mirror. A second door led outside. At the back

45

was a closet-sized bathroom with a toilet and a little sink. She closed and locked the door.

It was after she'd finished washing her hands and was about to leave that she suddenly heard female voices on the other side of the closed door. Two women had apparently entered the bride's room.

"You have a lot of nerve showing up here! You seduce my husband and then you have the gall to come to his funeral?"

"I loved him more than you ever did!"

Claudia grew still as a statue. The first voice was obviously Jo Louise. The other voice sounded like Sue Ember's.

"Just because he gave in to temptation, doesn't mean he had feelings for you. He begged me to forgive him after I found you together."

"Glen and I were lovers in high school," Sue asserted. "Did you know?"

"Ridiculous! Why would he have been attracted to you?"

"At first it was because I was a minister's daughter. He liked that. But then he also liked my curvaceous figure. Unlike you, I have flesh on my bones. All I had to do was give him a glimpse of cleavage after the prom, and he was all over me. I gave him everything, and I didn't care if it was a sin. You may have snookered him into marriage. But after twenty-six years apart, he and I still craved each other. God wanted *me* to be with him, not you!"

"You scheming hussy!" Jo Louise hissed. "Hanging around the church late to catch him alone. Seducing him on the rug in his office! How vulgar."

"We were in the throes of mind-blowing passion when you had to walk in!"

"How could you bring him so low?" Jo Louise asked, her voice breaking.

"He should have married me, and I proved it to him."

"You're no better than a harlot! And now he's gone. He confessed how horribly guilty he felt."

There was silence for a moment as Claudia listened, not moving a muscle, afraid she'd give her presence away.

"You think he killed himself?" Sue asked. "Is that what you think?"

"The police haven't figured it out."

"Maybe you killed him," Sue said.

"You low class piece of filth!" Jo Louise shot back as organ music began to flow from the sanctuary.

Claudia heard the door slam, then footsteps and the door closed again. She waited a few minutes longer and then carefully opened the door she'd been hiding behind. The bride's room was empty. Instead of leaving through the door that led to the sanctuary, she went out the other door into the courtyard. Walking around to the church's front steps, she entered the back of the sanctuary where Steve O'Rourke was still standing. Tapping his shoulder, she motioned him to follow her.

When they were outdoors and out of anyone's earshot, she told him all she'd overheard in the bride's room.

"Sue seems to think his wife killed him," Claudia said. "He was cheating, so that would be a strong motive."

Steve raised his eyebrows in a thoughtful expression. "It's a reasonable theory to look into. Good sleuthing." With an appreciative smile, he raised his hand to her shoulder level and curled his fingers. "That deserves a fist bump."

With a shy grin, she tapped her fist to his.

Chapter 6: The Cabinet above the Kitchen Counter

On Monday afternoon, the lab results came in for Sue's cat. Dr. Chandler prescribed an antibiotic that only came in pill form. Claudia phoned Sue to tell her, feeling uncomfortable after the lurid conversation she'd overheard in the bride's room.

"You'll come over and give Knickerbocker the pill, like you said?" Sue asked.

"Sure. Will you be home after five-thirty when I get off work?"

"That's perfect. You can do that until the prescription's finished?"

"No problem," Claudia assured her, though in truth she wasn't eager to see Sue, knowing the tawdry details of her secret affair with their deceased pastor. But she'd promised, and she had to think of Knickerbocker's welfare, too.

At about quarter to six, Claudia stood on the porch of the brick bungalow where Sue lived and rang the bell. In half a minute, Sue opened the door, wearing jeans and a long denim shirt.

"Claudia." With a smile, Sue invited her in. "You're so sweet to do this for Knicky."

"You're welcome. It works best for me if we can put the cat on a counter or table to give him the pill." Claudia pulled a small plastic bottle out of her leather handbag. "I've got the prescription." She showed it to Sue. "Enrofloxacin."

Sue squinted at the label. "Glad you know how to pronounce it. I wouldn't have a clue."

Claudia chuckled.

"Why don't you go into the kitchen," Sue said, pointing to the back of the house. "I'll find Knicky. I think he's in the bedroom. Just hope the doorbell didn't make him hide under the bed."

"No hurry," Claudia said. "Say, can I have a glass of water? Had salty French fries at lunch, and now I'm thirsty."

"Glasses are in the cabinet above the kitchen counter."

Sue headed down a narrow hall. Claudia walked through the small living room, the dining room, and into the kitchen wallpapered in a pattern of quaint teapots. She set her handbag on the blue-tiled counter and reached up to open a white-painted cabinet. It was filled with a set of dishes, so she opened the next cabinet. The shelves were packed full with crackers, granola bars, breakfast cereals, and a box of coffee pods on the top shelf. Claudia closed the cabinet, still hunting for a glass.

Something made her pause and open the cabinet again. She looked up at the box of pods, which had *Amaretto Ambrosia* printed on it in yellow lettering, similar to the box she'd seen next to McGrath's espresso machine. She recalled that over lunch at the Bumblebee, Sue had said she hated coffee. Looking around the kitchen, Claudia saw no coffee machine of any kind.

Her breaths quickening, she turned to see if Sue was coming. No sign of her. Claudia took her cell phone from her handbag and with jittery fingers found the card Steve had given her.

She entered his number, growing anxious, her heart pounding as she listened to the phone ring.

"O'Rourke."

"It's Claudia. I'm at Sue Ember's house." She gave him the address. "There's a box of the exact same pods that McGrath used," she told him in a low voice. "But Sue hates coffee and there's no machine here—"

"Found him," Sue said, carrying Knickerbocker into the kitchen. She stopped in her tracks as she saw Claudia on the phone. Sue looked up at the top shelf of the open cabinet. "Who are you talking to?"

"A . . . a co-worker at the clinic," Claudia improvised.

Sue dropped her cat onto the kitchen table. "Hang up," she told Claudia.

"W-why?"

"You're calling the cops aren't you?" Sue yanked open a drawer near the sink and pulled out a meat-carving knife. She advanced toward Claudia holding the knife in a threatening way. "Hang up and put the phone down!" she ordered in a strong voice.

Knickerbocker jumped from the table and fled.

"Okay. No need for a knife." Claudia pretended to end the call and then set the phone on the

51

counter. She stood in front of it, hoping Sue wouldn't see that it was still on.

"So I have coffee pods. It doesn't mean anything."

"But you don't have a machine." Claudia worked to keep her voice calm as she eyed the big knife in Sue's hand.

"That doesn't mean I killed Glen." Sue's face went red, then paled.

"If you didn't kill him, why are you holding a knife on me?"

Sue didn't seem to process Claudia's question. "I loved him."

"I know. I overheard your conversation with Jo Louise in the bride's room. You were having an affair with him."

"You heard . . . ?" Tears flooded Sue's eyes. "He was supposed to be mine. Ever since high school."

"You always said the man you loved in high school died."

"I had to think of him as dead," Sue said in an earnest, broken voice, as though needing to unburden herself. "We went steady. But senior year I could see he was losing interest. So I offered myself on prom night. My first experience. His, too. It was heaven. But the next day he apologized for sinning with me. And then he stopped seeing me. He went off to divinity school and I never heard from him. Broke my heart. I had to think of him as dead to me, especially after I found out he married some other minister's daughter. Jo Louise," she said with spite.

Claudia kept an eye on the knife Sue kept wildly brandishing, gesturing as she talked. But Claudia wanted to keep her talking. "So you didn't see him again for years?"

"Twenty-six years. And then, as if God had planned it, I was on the Pastor Nominating Committee and his resume came in. So I talked him up, convinced the committee to choose him. I was thrilled the first day I saw him at church. He recognized me and smiled. Jo Louise was on his arm, but I wasn't going to let her stand in my way." Sue's expression grew sullen as she spoke of Jo Louise.

"So you started volunteering in the church office to be near him?" Claudia prompted.

"I had to start slow. But before long, I had him in the palm of my hand. He likes a well-endowed body and Jo Louise is such a stick. The last time we made love, Jo Louise saw us. She had a fit!" Angry tears crumpled Sue's face. "She spoiled everything, that skinny little witch!"

"So what happened?" Claudia asked.

"The next day, he phoned and told me he couldn't see me anymore, to stay away. He chose Jo Louise over me! I couldn't believe it. I told him how I worked so hard to get the Pastor Nominating Committee to choose him. He owed me. I said we have such a deep passion for each other, why

53

doesn't he leave her and marry me? He said it would never happen, that I was delusional!"

"Must have been painful," Claudia said.

"It was horrible. Like he'd stuck this knife in my stomach!" She held the knife higher. "I couldn't let him get away with using me. I asked him to meet me early the next morning in his office. I put on a tragic voice and told him I needed to apologize for seducing him, for the sake of my immortal soul. He agreed. I bought the coffee. Snuck some cyanide from the factory, put it in a pod, hid it in my pocket and went to see him. No one else was around. I went in all abject and guilty, like I was going to tell him how sorry I was. But first I said I'd make his coffee for him. I pulled the pod out of my pocket and pretended to take it out of his box. The machine did its work. As he drank from the cup, I told him I always loved him and always would. But I wasn't about to let him reject me for Jo Louise. He started to feel sick and fell to his knees. He begged me to call 911. But I walked out and pulled the door closed. I . . . " she swallowed, "I couldn't watch him die. I left and drove away."

Claudia was feeling sick herself hearing Sue's description of how she'd committed murder. Still, Claudia needed to pull herself together to ask, "How did you get the cyanide into the pod?"

"Remember when Knickerbocker had that ear infection a few years ago?" Sue spoke to Claudia as someone would confide in an old friend. "I had to give him a liquid med that I squirted into his mouth.

54

I still had the little applicator and filled it with cyanide. I punctured the top of the pod with a pin, and pushed the tip of the applicator into the hole. It was easy. So easy." She nodded in a wistful way. "And now he's gone. Glen really is dead." Sue's tone had grown melancholy and she'd lowered the knife to her side.

Claudia wondered if she should try to grab the knife. Suddenly there was pounding at the front door. And then even louder pounding at the back door off the kitchen. Steve kicked the door in, entered and grabbed Sue, extracting the knife from her hand. Uniformed police came in and cuffed her.

As Claudia breathed a sigh of relief, Steve set his hands on Claudia's shoulders. "You okay?"

She nodded. "I hoped you'd hear what was going on." She turned to see her cell phone still on the counter.

"Smart gal," he said.

Meanwhile, one of the officers read Sue the Miranda rights. They began to lead her away, but she turned to Claudia. "Will you take care of Knicky?"

"Of course," Claudia assured her. "I'll take him to my house. Give him his medicine."

A tear slid down Sue's face as the cops kept hold of her. "And adopt him?"

"Sure."

"I wouldn't have hurt you, Claudia."

"I know, Sue. I know."

While Steve collected the knife and the box of coffee pods as evidence, Claudia found Sue's cat carrier in a closet. She looked for Knickerbocker and discovered him hiding under the bed. After talking to him softly for a minute, the big, fluffy, grey and brown Maine Coon came out. The cat knew her from visits to the clinic over the years and apparently had grown to trust her. She hugged him. "You're coming to live with me now." After putting him into the carrier, she walked through the house to the front door.

Steve seemed to be waiting for her, holding the knife and coffee pods in plastic evidence bags. "You're really taking the cat home with you?"

"Sue asked me to. I assume it's okay with the police?"

"Sure. We'd just have to bring him to a shelter. He's better off with you." He tilted his head a bit. "You don't mind adopting the cat?"

Claudia sighed. "It's been a long time since my last cat died. Not long after my husband passed away." She lifted her shoulders. "It's probably time to have a pet again. And Knickerbocker is a very sweet cat. I'll give him his medicine and he'll be fine."

Steve's eyes grew warm. "I'm sure he will be. You're the ideal cat mom."

#

The following Sunday morning, Claudia felt a reluctance to attend church after all that had happened. She'd skipped the previous Sunday. But

Amy had told her that the Chicago Presbytery had sent an experienced minister to act as first responder in the crisis. So she went into the church and sat in the last row. Up ahead she could see Amy and Larry in a pew on the left, midway up the aisle.

Claudia was reading the program for the service, when a man sat down beside her. She turned to say hello and saw it was Steve.

"You're coming to our church?" she said with a smile.

"Thought I'd give it a try," he told her. "Some of the members here are very nice." His eyes twinkled as he gazed at her.

"Glad you think so," she replied.

"By the way, you look fine in regular clothes."

Claudia looked down at her corduroy jacket and plaid skirt. "Thanks, but what do you mean?"

"No cartoon cats."

She laughed.

"Not that you didn't look awfully cute in your clinic outfit."

Claudia still chuckled as she felt her cheeks grow warm. She glanced away and happened to see Amy looking back at them across the pews.

Amy winked and gave Claudia a thumbs up.

Novella II

THE WINGED WITNESS

Chapter 1: "Shut up, Hal!"

Monday morning at the Briarwood Cat Clinic seemed even more harried than usual to veterinary technician Claudia Bailey. Maybe because Claudia had slept fitfully the night before, wondering, worrying, if it was possible she could find perfect love again. At age thirty-nine. Did all youngish widows question themselves this way?

Working with white-haired Dr. August Chandler, proud grandfather of three, in the clinic's treatment room, Claudia heard the squawk of a parrot out in the waiting area.

"Guess we know who's here," she joked to the highly-regarded veterinarian as she held a big tabby still while he cleaned out the cat's ears and applied a medication.

"Ethel and Tom Radek?" he replied with a smile. "Everywhere Tom goes, that African Grey

58

sits on his shoulder. Saw them out for a walk along the old railroad path the other day. The parrot took flight, then landed on Tom's shoulder again, so its wings aren't clipped. I was glad to see he had a harness and leash on the bird. How's their cat?"

"Ethel called first thing this morning," Claudia told him. "She said Jasmine was throwing up all weekend, and now the cat has stopped eating and drinking."

"That's not good," Dr. Chandler replied with a concerned sigh. "I'm finished with Buster, here. You can put the Radeks in an exam room. Do your prelim."

Claudia brought Buster back to his "mom" in one of the clinic's two small exam rooms, informing her that Dr. Chandler would talk to her about Buster's ear infection. She entered the waiting room with its wood bench, walls painted a cat's-eye shade of green, and big windows admitting the bright sunlight of a clear winter's day. It had snowed the night before all over Chicagoland, and the old-town heart of suburban Briarwood looked especially picturesque.

Ethel and Tom, who appeared to be in their sixties, sat in the corner. Their Himalayan, Jasmine, lay in her cat carrier on the bench next to Ethel. The medium-size parrot with grey feathers, a black beak, and bright red tail, sat on the bald-headed man's shoulder, its claws digging into his blue wool sweater. The bird's silver-colored harness matched its feathers.

"Hello," the bird said as Claudia approached.

"Hello," Claudia replied, chuckling as the parrot turned its head to eye her sideways. She looked at Ethel, whose lined face appeared grim beneath her thick salt-and-pepper bangs. "So how's Jasmine?"

"She's gotten very quiet," Ethel said in a grave manner. Her naturally strong voice grew imperative. "You know how she usually carries on when we bring her here. Wish this clinic was open on Sunday."

Claudia picked up the cat carrier. "Let's go into the second exam room."

The Radeks followed.

After setting the carrier onto the small room's stainless steel exam table, Claudia carefully pulled out Jasmine. The cat objected with a weak mew as Ethel and Tom took seats on the provided chairs. The Himalayan's blue eyes, usually so bright against her dark, seal-point face, were half-closed.

"She does seem listless," Claudia observed. "How long since she's eaten?"

"Friday morning," Ethel said. "And she hasn't gone near her water bowl."

"She hasn't wanted to drink from a faucet either," Tom said. "She likes to jump on the kitchen sink and meow for us to turn on the water."

"Meow," the parrot said.

"Can't you keep him quiet?" Ethel asked her husband with irritation.

"Shh, Hal." Tom brought his hand to his shoulder so the bird could step onto his fist. He gently ruffled the feathers on Hal's head, which the parrot seemed to enjoy.

Claudia had gotten out a thermometer and lifted the cat's thickly furred tail to take her temperature. As this took a minute, she chatted.

"You have a new hairstyle, don't you, Ethel?"

The thin, angular lady, dressed in wool pants, boots and a Fair Isle sweater, smiled. She fluffed her chin length hair. "I went to a different beauty parlor I heard about. Haven't worn bangs since I was a teenager, so it's kind of fun."

"I like it," Claudia said, pulling out the thermometer. "Oh, gosh, Jasmine's temperature is very low."

"No, really?" Ethel said with alarm. "I hadn't noticed."

"Her fur is so long and thick, you wouldn't have," Claudia assured her. She took the cat's pulse, observed its respiration, asked the couple some further questions about Jasmine and made notes for Dr. Chandler.

"What do you think might be wrong with her?" Ethel asked, leaning forward on the edge of her seat. "She's been my little pal for almost a dozen years."

Claudia knew it might be a fur ball obstruction, but it wasn't her place to diagnose. "Dr. Chandler will probably want an x-ray to evaluate what's going on. She may need to stay here overnight for observation or treatment."

"Sounds expensive," Tom mumbled, lifting the bird to his shoulder again.

Ethel turned to him. "You always think like an accountant. Our beloved kitty is sick!"

"Well," he said quietly, "I *was* an accountant."

"You're only semi-retired," she continued. Her sharp voice had a natural hectoring quality. "You still get a paycheck. And when the court decides in your favor, money definitely won't be a problem." She turned to Claudia. "Cruella de Ville, the blood-sucking trophy wife—widow, I should say—of Tom's father is contesting the will. But we have a good lawyer. We'll inherit what we're entitled to. Tom's such a worry-wart."

As Tom looked down at the tiled floor, Claudia nodded, unsure what to say.

The parrot spoke up before she could. "Smart bird. Smart bird."

"Oh, shut up, Hal!" Ethel exclaimed.

"Shut up, Hal," the bird instantly repeated, puffing out its feathers.

Tom petted the bird and spoke softly to it. "It's okay. She didn't mean it."

"Dr. Chandler will come in soon," Claudia told them as she stroked Jasmine. "He'll do a thorough exam."

A while later, Dr. Chandler carried Jasmine back to the treatment room and asked Claudia to take the cat's blood pressure. While she wrapped the white cuff around the cat's front leg, he said, "I felt a blockage in her colon. So we need an x-ray, maybe an ultrasound."

Claudia sighed a half-minute later as she read the monitor that showed the blood pressure reading. "It's so low. She's badly dehydrated."

"Right. She'll probably need surgery today," the veterinarian said. "Let's get the x-ray, then wrap her in a blanket and use the warm air blower to increase her temperature. We'll insert an IV catheter to get fluid into the kidneys to raise her blood pressure."

"Will the Radeks be okay with all that? Tom seemed concerned about the cost."

"I haven't given them an estimate yet," he replied.

"Oh, boy," Claudia said under her breath, knowing the sum would total thousands of dollars.

A half hour later, Claudia saw the Radeks sitting in the waiting room. Ethel looked distraught.

Claudia walked up to them. "Jasmine seems to be feeling more comfortable. We've warmed her up and her blood pressure is getting back to normal."

"But the vet says she needs surgery," Ethel said. "She's an older cat. Will she survive?"

"Dr. Chandler has done many, many surgeries. He's rarely lost a patient."

"If she survives," Ethel went on, "how do we take care of her? I comb her, but she still got this fur ball blockage. What if the same thing happens, and she has to have surgery again?"

Claudia listened as Ethel babbled on in an emotional outpouring, inventing awful scenarios about Jasmine's future. Tom, meanwhile, had a blank expression on his face while Hal sat on his shoulder.

"Well, one thing you can do," Claudia interrupted Ethel, "is have Jasmine get the lion cut. That way she won't ingest so much fur. We have a groomer here."

"I've heard of that," Ethel said. "But then she'll look like a little lion? She won't be my fluffy Jasmine anymore." She turned to her husband. "What do you think, Tom?"

He didn't respond.

"Tom? Are you listening?"

He lifted his chin. "Huh?"

"Turn up your hearing aid," Ethel snapped.

"It's on," he said.

"If Jasmine survives the surgery, should we give her the lion cut?"

"What's a lion cut?"

Ethel closed her eyes and shook her head. "You're impossible! When I'm talking, try listening for a change."

"Tom? Tom?" Hal said, suddenly flapping his wings. "Tom, you listening?"

Claudia needed to get back to her work. "Did Dr. Chandler give you the estimate of what the surgery will cost?"

"Yes, he did," Tom replied. "We're waiting to sign the paper to go ahead." He glanced at his watch. "Will that take long?"

Claudia looked toward the reception desk. "I'm sure they're printing it up now."

"I was hoping to go help out Eleanor," Tom told his wife.

"Eleanor is clever at coming up with stuff for you to do," Ethel said in a dour tone.

"She's got a bad back," Tom replied matter-of-factly. "She needs help around her house."

Trudy Avery, the clinic's office manager, a plump middle-aged blond, approached with a document in her hand. "Here's the rundown of the cost of the surgery, the x-ray and ultrasound, the blood panel and urine tests, and the medications. She'll probably need to be here for two or three nights which entails a boarding fee."

Tom took the paper and perused it. "Holy cow," he said as he accepted the pen from her.

"Sign it," Ethel insisted. "Jasmine's worth every penny."

Tom smiled. "Yes, she is." He signed the document.

"I'll keep in touch and let you know how Jasmine's doing," Claudia said. She walked back to the treatment room, where except for the occasional meowing of several confined cats, she enjoyed a few minutes of quiet attending Jasmine. She wondered how Tom Radek had the patience to live with a high strung, verbose wife who constantly demanded his attention.

#

"So," Amy said, after the waitress had taken their lunch order, "anything percolating between you and the handsome Detective O'Rourke? I've seen him sitting with you at church every Sunday."

Claudia glanced out the large front window of the quaint Bumblebee Café where she and Amy Kopecky met for lunch every few weeks. Across the street stood the picturesque First Presbyterian Church with its old-fashioned bell tower, where they both were members.

"Steve and I are just friends," Claudia said.

"He hasn't asked you on a date or anything?"

"No." Claudia took a nonchalant tone. "The last few Sundays he's taken me to The Old Mill for brunch."

"He did?" Amy leaned forward with excitement, her red curls bouncing.

"Brunch after church isn't a date," Claudia argued, feeling inexplicably uneasy. "It's just where we go after the service is over."

"Come on. The Old Mill? That's a really nice restaurant." Amy's green eyes sparkled. "It's not like you walk across the street to come here for a burger. Maybe he's trying to impress you."

Claudia shrugged.

"And I've noticed on Sundays you don't wear your hair tied back with a barrette."

66

Self-consciously touching the tortoise-shell clip that held her long blond hair at the nape of her neck, Claudia said, "So what?"

"Don't be obtuse," Amy told her. "In high school you wore your hair loose over your shoulders. You used to twist a curl around your finger when you flirted with boys."

Claudia drew her brows together in irritation. "I don't do that anymore."

"Still," Amy insisted, "letting your hair go free makes you look feminine and available."

"It does?" She stared at her friend, feeling a little dumb-struck. "That wasn't my intention. I'm just trying to look nice for church."

"You've had your hair tied back ever since Peter died," Amy pointed out. "You sure it's not because a tall, seriously gorgeous detective is obviously interested in you? Before you met Steve, you said that you were open to the idea of dating again."

Claudia did remember saying that. The memory of Peter, Claudia's deceased husband, flew through her mind. Before he died of leukemia, Peter had told her he hoped she would marry again, that she shouldn't feel she was being untrue to him. Peter didn't want her to be alone, especially since they hadn't had children.

"I don't know." Claudia felt antsy, but didn't know why. "Can't we talk about something else?"

Amy studied her. "What's going on with you?"

Claudia sighed. "Nothing. I've only known Steve for three months."

"That's way long enough to start dating him."

"Amy, it's my life and my decision."

"Okay," Amy said in a resigned tone. "But even Larry thought Steve looks at you with a certain glow in his eyes," she added, referring to her husband.

"Don't be silly," Claudia said with increasing impatience. "Find some other subject to harp on."

Amy's head went back. "Pardon me!"

"Sorry," Claudia murmured.

Amy took a long breath. "How are things at cat rehab?"

Claudia relaxed. "Fine. Had an emergency surgery this morning. Fur ball blockage."

"How's the patient?"

"She went through the surgery very well," Claudia said. "So I called her owner with the good news. But the woman—Ethel is her name—got so emotional. Couldn't stop thanking me, and then worrying how to take care of the cat. Talked my ear off. I had a hard time ending the call. I think her husband just tunes her out sometimes. What else can he do?" Claudia shook her head. "Not all marriages turn out as well as yours has. Or mine, until I was widowed."

"Is that why you're in denial about Steve O'Rourke's interest in you?"

"In denial?" Claudia sighed in exasperation. "How did we get from talking about a cat surgery to Steve? Your mind sure makes great leaps!"

Amy nodded, unfazed. "And yours is stuck in the past."

#

About six p.m., before going home, Claudia decided to call Ethel again to reassure her that Jasmine was still doing well. She punched in the number and waited while the phone rang several times. Then the answering machine came on with Tom's voice saying please leave a message.

"Hi Ethel and Tom. This is Claudia from the cat clinic. Jasmine is—"

"Hello? Claudia?"

The abrupt male voice surprised her. He didn't sound at all like Tom.

"Y-yes, Claudia Bailey calling to speak to Ethel about her cat."

"Really?" the man replied in an amazed manner. "This is Steve."

Claudia blinked. "Steve? Why are you there?"

"I'm on a case, investigating a murder."

Claudia felt her cheeks grow cold as blood drained from her face. "Who was murdered?"

"Tom Radek. Stabbed." Steve paused. "Say, do you know how to take care of a parrot?"

Chapter 2: Bingo

"I've interviewed Ethel," Steve, looking official in his suit and tie, told Claudia. They were enjoying the meatloaf special at the Bumblebee Café.

Claudia assumed this was not a dinner "date." Steve had suggested they meet for a bite to eat. He'd said that because she knew the Radeks, she might be an asset in his investigation. Still in shock that Tom had been murdered only hours after she'd seen him at the clinic, she earnestly wanted to help.

"What did Ethel say?" she asked.

"Her story is that she went to play bingo at a senior center in Wheaton, and when she came home she found her husband dead on the floor. She called 911."

"Does Ethel have any idea who killed him?"

"She sounds certain that the murderer must be Tom's father's widow, who's been contesting his dad's will."

Claudia nodded. "She mentioned that at the clinic this morning. She called the woman Cruella de Ville. But Ethel was sure that their lawyer would win the court case and Tom would inherit."

"Cruella de Ville?" Steve laughed, causing pleasing crinkles to form around his brown eyes. "The stepmother's name is Roberta Radek."

"Ethel has a way of exaggerating things," Claudia said. "You should hear how she carries on about her sick cat. I've been trying to reassure her the cat will recover and live a healthy life."

Steve paused while their waitress refilled their cups of coffee. "Haven't been able to reach Roberta. What was the matter with the cat?"

"Fur ball blockage. Himalayans have tons of long fur. I assisted with the surgery this morning."

Steve's eyes widened with what looked like admiration. "You help do surgeries?"

"Monitoring the anesthesia and the cat's vitals. Handing Dr. Chandler the scalpel and suture packet. Things like that."

"I'm impressed."

Claudia looked down, feeling self-conscious, but in an uplifting way. It was odd, but whenever she was with Steve, she felt positive and happy. It was when she was away from him that doubts about her budding feelings crept into her thoughts.

She reminded herself to focus on the murder. "It will be hard for Ethel to live in that house after seeing her husband's body, knowing he was stabbed to death."

Steve shook his head, his eyes darkening. "It's a crime scene. There's a lot of blood. The knife must have hit an artery or maybe his heart. She's staying at a hotel tonight. And the parrot is at our police station. The bird has blood on its wing, so we needed to take it in as evidence. Have the blood tested, see if it's Tom's or maybe the murderer's."

"That poor bird," Claudia said. "His name is Hal."

Steve half-smiled. "So that's why the bird keeps saying, 'Shut up, Hal.' He's a noisy creature. He also keeps repeating, 'No, don't!' in a shrieking tone. Makes me wonder if that's what Tom said to his killer. Wish the parrot could tell us who stabbed Tom. Hal must have witnessed the whole thing."

"How awful," Claudia murmured. "Did you find some parrot food at the house for him?"

"One of our men found some in the pantry, so we took it with us along with the big birdcage. Managed to catch him and put him in it. How often do you have to feed a parrot?"

Claudia lifted her shoulders. "I'm not sure. There might be directions on the bag of food."

"Good idea." Steve finished off his last bite of meatloaf and took a sip of coffee.

Claudia wasn't so hungry anymore and pushed away her half-finished plate. "When will you be able to give the bird back to Ethel?"

"We'll need to keep it for a few days." Steve's eyes twinkled as he looked at her. "The bird could be a flight risk."

Shoulders shaking, Claudia laughed at his joke.

He grinned. "I'm glad to see you smile. It's been a rough day for you."

She nodded. "Tom was a very nice man. I don't know why anyone would want to kill him. Where is Ethel now?"

"At the Briarwood Arms Hotel. She said the hotel won't allow pets, so she can't take the bird as long as she's there."

"Will she ever want to go back to her home?" Claudia wondered aloud, feeling troubled.

"Good question, especially if she's the murderer."

"What?" Claudia stared at him. "You think she . . . ?"

His eyes met hers, unblinking. "The spouse is usually the first to come under suspicion."

Steve's low voice had fallen into an uncompromising monotone. This was the same way he'd spoken to her the day she first met him, when he'd questioned her about the murder of the church minister whose body she'd discovered. Steve's deadpan detective manner still unnerved her just a bit.

Claudia swallowed. "But Ethel told you she was playing bingo at a senior center. Can't that be checked out?"

"You bet. I'll be heading to Wheaton after we're done here." Raising his eyebrows, he took a softer tone. "Want to come?"

Claudia smiled. "Me? On an official investigation?"

"You know Ethel. Might be helpful."

#

Claudia thought it would be fun to ride in a police car instead of Steve's personal car, the blue Chevy Volt he drove to church and to take her to

73

The Old Mill afterward. She was disappointed when he opened the passenger door of an unmarked black Charger.

She chuckled as she got in the passenger seat. "Didn't Columbo drive a Peugeot convertible? You have an ordinary Dodge?"

"I don't wear a rumpled raincoat either," he quipped as he shut the door.

"You do look more together," she said as he got in behind the wheel. She eyed his camel overcoat and plaid wool scarf.

Then she noticed police radio equipment by the dashboard and a spotlight on the driver side mirror. The windows had a heavy tint, too.

He drove to the senior center in Wheaton, about twenty minutes away. They entered the one-story brick building and walked around a group of people seated for a lecture given by a woman in a nurse's uniform. From what bits she heard, Claudia deduced that the subject was prescription drugs.

Steve led the way toward the back of the large room, where there was a door to an office. He walked up to the fortyish, bespectacled man behind the desk and showed his badge.

"Detective Steve O'Rourke, Briarwood Police. I need to ask a few questions."

The man behind the desk stood. "I'm John Axelrod. How can I help?"

"You have a bingo game here on Monday afternoons at three o'clock?"

"Yes, the first and third Mondays of the month."

"So one took place today?"

"I supervised it myself."

Steve opened up a tablet he was carrying and quickly thumbed the keys to bring up a photo. "Do you recognize this woman? Was she here this afternoon for bingo?"

Axelrod took the tablet and squinted at the photo on the screen, adjusting his glasses. "Oh, she was here. Definitely. She's one of our regulars. Seems like a nice lady." He looked at Steve. "Has she gone missing or something?" he asked with concern.

"Her husband was murdered. We need to confirm her whereabouts."

"Oh, my goodness."

"You recall her name?" Steve asked.

Axelrod looked up at the ceiling. "Well, it starts with an E, I think? I remember faces better than names, I'm afraid."

"Ethel?" Claudia suggested.

The man nodded. "Yeah, that sounds right. Ethel."

"Last name Radek?" Steve asked.

"Oh, I never can remember last names." He shook his head.

Steve took back the tablet, then held out his hand to Axelrod. "You've been helpful. Thanks."

"How awful her husband was murdered." He shook Steve's hand. "Hope you find who did it."

As they walked back to the unmarked police car in the parking lot, Claudia said to Steve, "I'm glad Ethel's no longer a suspect. I wonder why she drives to Wheaton for bingo? There's a senior center in Briarwood."

"Good point," Steve said, looking thoughtful.

"Maybe it has bingo on a different night, and Mondays are more convenient for her." Claudia sighed and looked at Steve. "Are there any other possible culprits, besides Roberta Radek?"

"Ethel says one of their neighbors, Ed Lynch, has been complaining about the squawking parrot. Threatened to wring the bird's neck. She thinks he might have come over while she was gone to harm the bird. Maybe Tom got into a fight with Lynch and wound up dead."

"But the parrot's still alive," Claudia said.

"Another good observation," Steve agreed.

"Unless Ed Lynch got so spooked at having stabbed Tom, he ran out and forgot about the parrot. Is there a murder weapon at the scene?"

"Haven't found one so far," Steve said. "The autopsy will help determine what we should look for."

As they drove back to Briarwood, Claudia grew thoughtful. "Do you like being a detective?"

"I like solving puzzles and putting away criminals. Getting justice for victims is rewarding."

"Is your job dangerous?" she asked in a careful way. "Do you carry a gun?"

As he drove, he turned his head to her briefly and nodded. "Does that bother you?"

She drew in a long breath. "I suppose you must," she replied in an agreeable tone. But she didn't like it. Her husband had died too young. Did she want to grow emotionally attached to another man who might meet an untimely death?

Claudia looked out her side window at the passing street lights and headlights shining dreamlike in the darkness, and shut the unsettling question out of her mind.

Chapter 3: What Could Possibly Go Wrong?

The following Saturday, Claudia attended the funeral service for Tom Radek, held at the Holy Trinity Episcopal Church. The medium-sized church with tall, narrow, stained glass windows was only about half full. The closed coffin sat on a bier at the front.

Claudia slid into a pew toward the back and was soon joined by Steve, who had told her he planned to attend. She knew from past experience that he found a murder victim's funeral to be a good place to scope out possible suspects.

"How are you?" Steve asked as he sat down next to her.

"Okay." She only half-smiled. "I don't like funerals."

"I know. They always remind me of my wife's memorial service, even though years have passed. Same for you?"

Claudia nodded, thinking of Peter's funeral. "I feel for Ethel. She's been dabbing her face with a handkerchief. The murder has been in the paper. Must be hard for her."

Steve tilted his head and looked toward the front pew where Ethel sat. "All dressed in black. Looks the picture of a grieving widow alright."

"Has she gone back to her house yet? Her cat is doing well. We've been boarding her until Ethel can take her home."

"She's still at the hotel. The bloodstained rug at the house will need to be cleaned or replaced. The hotel's letting her stay at half rate." Steve seemed preoccupied looking at a group of men and women sitting close together, filling a pew across the aisle. "Those are Tom's co-workers from Briarwood Certified Public Accountants." Steve kept his voice low as he motioned toward them. "I went to their office the morning after the murder to ask some questions. Didn't learn much. They all seemed genuinely shocked at the news. Tom only worked there part-time the last two years, being semi-retired. He'd been a partner in the firm."

"The brunette sitting on the aisle looks distraught," Claudia whispered. She noticed the young woman's hand trembling as she pushed back her long hair.

"Mia Wilson. She went pale when I told the employees Tom was stabbed to death. Mia was Tom's secretary. I was afraid she'd pass out. She's another partner's secretary, too. Greg Owen, the big grey-haired guy next to her."

"She seems very nervous," Claudia said with concern. "Or scared."

Steve looked in Mia Wilson's direction, his eyes intent. "You're right. Her posture is rigid, like she's afraid to move." He shifted his gaze to Claudia. "You're very observant. You were really

79

helpful solving the murder of your church minister, too."

Claudia smiled and shrugged. "That was mostly luck, being at the right place at the right time."

He looked at her with admiration. "More than luck, I think."

Claudia felt warm under his gaze, liking his attention and yet feeling unsettled. Should she flirt back? Was she ready for where that might lead?

Just then, Claudia noticed a woman using a walker making her way slowly down the side aisle. She wore sunglasses, a long grey overcoat, a knit white beret over her hair and a scarf around her neck partly covering her face. The woman reached the pew behind Ethel as the priest began the service. She laid her hand on Ethel's shoulder, and Ethel turned around and nodded to her.

"A friend?" Claudia whispered to Steve, whose eyes seemed to be glued on the woman, too. "Or maybe a cousin or aunt?"

"Don't know." He subtly pointed to a man sitting a few pews ahead of them. "By the way, that's Ed Lynch, the neighbor who Ethel suspected. The guy she said threatened to wring the parrot's neck. He was out of town the day of the murder. Hotel and restaurant receipts prove it."

"Well that's one less suspect," Claudia said. "So, how's Hal doing?"

Steve nodded in a hesitant way. "Um, okay. I may need to talk to you about that later."

Mystified, and growing suspicious, Claudia did not reply. She remained quiet through the rest of the service, as did Steve.

#

Claudia and Steve drove in their separate cars to the cemetery to observe the burial. The grass in between the rows of gravestones was covered with snow slowly melting under a sunny sky. They stayed about fifteen yards back from the small group gathered around the coffin, where the priest gave a few final remarks and said a prayer. The woman with the walker stood near Ethel, head bowed.

Claudia noticed that Mia was the only person from Tom's office who came to view the interment. She stood back from the mourners around the coffin, too, but some distance away from Claudia and Steve.

"Look, she's openly weeping," Claudia whispered to Steve. "I feel bad for her."

"I wonder why." Steve's expression had grown puzzled. "You're an empathetic person. Why don't you go up to her and ask if she's all right. I'll follow."

His request surprised Claudia, but she quietly began walking toward Mia.

"Excuse me, but I see you're upset," Claudia softly told the young woman whose eyes were red and wet. "Are you okay?"

Mia looked startled. "Oh . . . sure. Tom was . . . a wonderful, upstanding person."

"I knew him and liked him, too. I'm Claudia Bailey. He and his wife brought their cat to the clinic where I work."

Mia shook her head. "Tom didn't deserve what happened to him. He was only trying to do the right thing."

Claudia glanced at Steve, who had stepped up beside her. Steve's intent look silently urged her to continue.

"The right thing?" Claudia repeated. "Was something wrong?"

"He'd discovered . . . ." Mia stopped short. "I can't talk about that."

Steve leaned toward her. "Will you be in trouble if you do?"

Mia's pale blue eyes widened. She stared up at him dumbfounded. "You're that detective. I shouldn't have said anything." She turned to walk away.

"Wait," Steve said. "Please. We need to find Tom's murderer. If you know anything that might be helpful, you'd be honoring Tom's memory by telling us. The police can protect you, if necessary."

Mia paused, looking at the ground as if transfixed for a long moment. Her taut expression changed and she faced Steve and Claudia. "But I'm scared. My boss is . . . not a nice guy. Harassment comes natural to him. It was a great place to work until I became Greg Owen's secretary."

"I'm so sorry," Claudia said. "He intimidates you?"

82

"He said if I told anyone, he'd have me fired."
Mia's hand shook as she wiped wetness from her
face. But her demeanor had become more resolute.
"I can't go on this way." She looked up at Steve.
"Tom found out that Greg is embezzling one of
Tom's former clients, a power tool manufacturing
company."

"Go on," Steve encouraged her.

"I'd left work at five o'clock one night. I was in
the parking lot when I realized I'd forgotten my
half-sandwich from lunch. So I went back in and
walked to our little kitchen to get it out of the
refrigerator. On the way I passed Greg's office and
heard them arguing. Greg had taken over the
account from Tom. I heard Tom say that the owner
came to him to ask about the company's financial
reports. The balances seemed out of line with past
reports. Tom looked into it. He told Greg he knew
he was embezzling. Tom said he could prove it and
advised Greg to come clean or he'd report him to
the police. Greg's going through a nasty divorce. He
probably needs money. He and Tom got into a
shouting match. And then Greg saw I was in the
hallway and could hear them."

Mia took a deep breath and lifted her hand to
her forehead as if she felt lightheaded.

"Are you okay?" Claudia asked.

Mia nodded. She looked at Steve. "Tom
ordered Greg to leave me alone, but Greg
threatened me anyway. Took me by the shoulders
and shook me hard, said I'd be out of work and that

would be the least of my worries if I told anyone. When you came to the office and said Tom had been murdered, I didn't have to guess who could have done it. He probably killed Tom to keep him quiet."

While Steve asked Mia to come to the station and make a statement, Claudia noticed the quiet ceremony around the coffin had ended. She felt she should say something to Ethel. Claudia headed in her direction as the lady with the walker who had stood next to Ethel slowly made her way toward the narrow cemetery road where people had parked their cars.

"I'm so sorry," Claudia told Ethel, taking her gloved hand. "Tom was a fine man."

Ethel nodded and murmured a thank-you. "How's Jasmine?"

"Jasmine is doing very well. She'll need to be on several medications for about a week, but you can take her home."

Ethel shook her head. "The hotel won't allow pets. And I don't know how I can live in my house again after . . . . I'll need to find an apartment or condo and sell the house. But all that's too much to think about right now."

"I understand." Claudia hesitated, thinking twice about offering to help. But she found herself saying, "I can take Jasmine home with me and give her the medications."

Ethel's hazel eyes widened in appreciation. "Oh, would you? I'm no good at giving a cat a pill.

And if she's with you, she won't be left there when the clinic is closed overnight and on Sunday."

"Someone comes in to check on our 'guest' cats on Sunday. But I know you'd feel better if she was looked after at my house. I already have a cat I adopted, but I can keep them in separate rooms."

"You're a godsend, Claudia. Can I come and visit Jasmine now and then? I mean, until I'm settled in a new place."

"Sure, call me and we'll figure out a convenient time." She gave Ethel her number.

Steve strode up to them. Claudia noticed Mia walking to her car.

Ethel turned to Steve. "Have you investigated Roberta?"

"Yes. Roberta Radek was at her dentist having a root canal at the time of the murder. Her dentist confirmed it."

Ethel twisted her mouth in annoyance. "I was sure it was her."

Claudia looked to Steve, wanting to tell Ethel what Mia had revealed. But she knew she should leave it to the detective to convey any details.

"Do you know Greg Owen?" Steve asked Ethel.

"Tom's partner? I've met him." Ethel appeared startled. "You think he did it?"

"Did Tom ever talk about a client being embezzled?"

Ethel's expression cleared. "Come to think of it, Tom did say he thought Greg was doing something underhanded. I didn't pay much attention. You think Greg murdered Tom to keep him from saying anything?"

"We're going to look into it."

"I have heard that Greg has a temper," Ethel said.

Steve paused. "So, we're done with your parrot. Our lab results show the blood on its wing matches your husband's. When can you take him?"

Ethel stepped backward. "I can't have that noisy bird in my hotel room. They don't allow any pets at all. Claudia's going to look after my cat until I'm settled in a new place."

Claudia gazed up at the clouds in the sky, anticipating what Steve would say next.

He turned to her. "Can you take care of the parrot, too?"

"I have little experience with birds," Claudia said.

"Well, none of us cops at the station do either. He's pulling out his feathers, squawking and talking constantly. Drives us nuts."

"Pulling out his feathers is a sign of stress," Claudia said. "He witnessed the murder of his favorite person and he's traumatized."

"Hal is talking a lot?" Ethel asked Steve. "What's he saying?"

"Mostly 'Shut up, Hal.' And also, 'No, don't!' in a harrowing screech."

Ethel seemed to grow slightly pale. "I'm very sorry if he's traumatized, but I can't take care of

him right now. Just feed him some parrot food.
He'll be fine."

At the clinic, Claudia had observed that Hal
was much more Tom's pet than Ethel's. "Okay, I'll
take Hal. Maybe he'll calm down when he sees
Jasmine."

Ethel smiled. "Why, you're right. Hal likes to
cuddle with Jasmine. They're friends. Oh, that's the
best of all worlds if you take them both. I'm very
appreciative, Claudia."

Claudia gave her a reluctant nod and
murmured, "You're welcome." *Two cats who don't
know each other and a frantic bird. What could
possibly go wrong?* She looked at her watch. "I'd
better get to the clinic. I told them I'd be in this
afternoon. Have to change into my scrubs."

Steve smiled at her, his eyes growing
whimsical. "I like your outfit with the cartoon cat
faces the best."

Claudia pressed her lips together, trying to look
annoyed, yet couldn't help but chuckle. "I know
you do. I wore them the day you met me and
interviewed me."

"An image I'll never forget," he said amiably,
his brown eyes earnest as they gazed into hers.

Claudia drove home to quickly change clothes,
choosing the cartoon cat tunic out of the several
scrubs she owned. She went to the clinic, still a little
disconcerted, not by the funeral and burial, but by
the way Steve made her feel—cherished, even

adored. She had the sensation of being a little high, like she'd drunk champagne.

And that, in turn, began to worry her. Her life had become placid and predictable. She'd grown to like it that way. Steve kept making ripples in her calm waters, which made her both excited and apprehensive.

At the end of the day, Claudia brought Jasmine, along with the cat's various medications, home with her. Fortunately Knickerbocker, the Maine Coon cat Claudia had adopted months ago, was fast asleep, curled up on Claudia's bed. She quietly crept past the bedroom with Jasmine in a cat carrier and went to the guest room. After closing the door, she opened up the carrier to let Jasmine out. At first the Himalayan seemed afraid to move, but after Claudia set out some cat food, a bowl of water, and a litter pan, Jasmine came out to sniff the food. Claudia sat down on the floor and petted her.

"You'll be safe here until you can go home with Ethel," she told the cat, who appreciatively licked her hand. How long would it be before Ethel found a new place to live? Claudia feared she'd get too attached to Jasmine if she kept the cat more than a few days.

Chapter 4: A Happy Reunion

As expected, that evening the doorbell rang. Knickerbocker was sleeping on the living room couch, but raised his head in alarm.

"It's okay," she told the Maine Coon as she hurried to open her front door.

Steve stood there carrying a big birdcage. Hal, the African Grey, flapped its wings inside the cage, making squawking parrot noises.

"Come on in," Claudia said.

"Thanks." Steve walked through the door into her living room. "Where do you want me to put Hal?"

"Shut up, Hal," the bird said.

"Well, I have Ethel's cat in the guest room. It's best to keep the two cats apart. Jasmine will only be here temporarily anyway. So why don't we put Hal in that room, too. He'll be near Jasmine, which might calm him down."

"Okay, lead the way."

Steve followed her to the guest bedroom, pristine from lack of use. The double bed was covered with a quilted spread. Bed stands with lamps stood on either side of the oak headboard. There was a comfortable easy chair in one corner, where Jasmine had curled up. The cat's blue eyes looked warily at Steve.

Claudia closed the door to make sure the two cats stayed separated. Knickerbocker might have already picked up Jasmine's scent.

"Where would you like the birdcage?" Steve asked.

Removing one of the lamps from a bed stand, she said, "How about here?"

He placed the cage where she indicated. "I brought the parrot food. I'll get it from my car."

During the few minutes he was gone, Claudia petted Jasmine and then walked up to the birdcage. "Hello, Hal," she said softly. Then she noticed the feathers down the front of his body were missing, leaving bare skin. "You're all discombobulated, aren't you? You'll be okay here. See Jasmine over there?" She stepped aside and walked over to the cat.

"Meow," Hal said.

Jasmine sat up, her eyes wide. Claudia wondered if she should let Hal out of the cage. Just then, Steve came in carrying the bag of food. Claudia closed the door behind him.

"Why don't we try letting Hal out?" she said. "Tom Radek always had him on his shoulder when they came to the clinic."

"Tom didn't worry about droppings?" Steve said.

"I guess not. I've only worked with cats since I got my veterinary technician's license. That was over fifteen years ago."

Steve shrugged. "Up to you. Sorry to impose the parrot on you like this. But you'd be better at figuring out how to take care of him than any of us at the station."

"Thanks for your confidence," she said, amused.

"Meow," Hal said, followed by, "Smart bird."

Claudia talked to the parrot in soothing tones a while longer, then opened the cage door.

The bird hesitated for a moment. Claudia raised her arm to the cage and Hal stepped out onto her forearm.

"Smart bird, Hal," she told him. Slowly she walked with the bird to the easy chair where Jasmine was sitting, round-eyed, watching them approach. All at once the bird took off from Claudia's arm and landed near Jasmine on the chair.

"His wings aren't clipped," Claudia observed. "Do you have his harness and leash?"

"Parrots can be leashed?" Steve seemed astonished. "Maybe they're still at the Radek house."

Hal started preening Jasmine's ear, which the cat didn't seem to mind.

Claudia glanced at Steve. "Looks like we're having a happy reunion."

He slipped his arm around her shoulders and gave her a quick hug. "You really understand animals. Thanks for doing this."

A bit disconcerted by the hug, Claudia asked, "Would you like some coffee?"

"Have you had supper yet?" he asked.

"Um, no. I was just going to have a frozen dinner."

"How about if I order a pizza for us?"

Claudia smiled. "Well, okay."

Steve took out his cell phone and speed dialed a number. "What do you like on your pizza?"

"How about chicken, spinach and mushrooms?"

He grinned. "Sounds healthy." In a moment he spoke into the phone and ordered a medium pizza with exactly the ingredients she suggested and gave Claudia's address.

After ending the call, he began to look around him. "Nice house. It's Tudor, isn't it? I noticed the arched front door. And it's brick."

"Yes. I inherited it from my parents." Claudia looked at Jasmine, who was curled on her side, the shaved area of her stomach showing from her surgery. The healing long dark line of her incision was just visible. But she seemed content with Hal hovering over her. "Should we leave them alone for a while?"

They entered the living room with its hardwood floor and large oval throw rug braided in yarns of green, burgundy and ivory, colors that went with the upholstered couch and two easy chairs. Steve stopped in front of Knickerbocker. The cat went up on its feet, about to bolt.

"This is Steve, Knicky," Claudia said, stroking the cat. "He's a good guy."

92

The big Maine Coon sat down, but his emerald eyes still looked wary.

"Is this Sue Ember's cat?" Steve asked. "She asked you to adopt him as we handcuffed her."

"He's gotten used to living with me. I write to Sue in prison. Send her pictures of him."

"Nice of you," Steve said. "Do you have other pets? I figured you for a cat lady."

Claudia smiled. "I had cats growing up and while I was married." She pointed to a bookcase in one corner, next to the brick fireplace. "There are all my cat figurines. Been collecting them since I was a kid. There are about fifty. And on the lower shelf are my boxes of cat jigsaw puzzles."

Steve walked up to the bookcase and looked over the figurines. "Do you have favorites?"

"The ones that are about four inches tall with flowery hats." She came up next to him and pointed at the five figurines she was describing.

"Very cute," he said. "You jump rope?" He pointed to the coiled rope on the floor near the bookcase.

She spread her hands. "Jumping rope and walking are what passes for my exercise routine."

"Seems to keep you fit. We have a workout room at the station." He turned and took a step to the oak fireplace mantle. Pointing to one of two silver-framed photos, he asked, "Your parents?"

"Vick and Claudia. I was named after my mom. They've both passed on."

"Brothers or sisters?"

She shook her head.

He picked up the remaining photo. "Your husband?"

"Yes, that's Peter." She gazed at the image of the handsome blond man she'd fallen in love with in high school. "That was taken on his thirtieth birthday. He died only two years later."

"Good looking fellow. What did he do for a living?"

"He was a stock broker. A fine businessman. Left me well-set." Claudia blinked to keep wetness from her eyes.

Steve quietly and carefully replaced the framed photo on the mantle. "Being widowed isn't easy," he murmured. "What happened to the cats you had while you were married?"

"They died, too. I lost the last one a few years ago." She showed him a needlepointed pillow on the easy chair. "This pillow I stitched looks like Taffy. She was an orange and white tabby. Somehow I hadn't felt like taking in a new cat. But then Knickerbocker needed a home, and Sue asked me, so . . . ." She smiled. "He's a very sweet cat. Older, so he sleeps a lot. Still pretty healthy though. Likes to be cuddled."

Steve nodded as he listened, but she sensed by his lowered gaze that he was mulling something over. Without looking at her, he asked, "Do you think you'd ever like to marry again?" He met her gaze. "You seem pretty self-sufficient."

The question took her by surprise coming from Steve. For years her friend Amy kept asking and hinting that she should look for a husband, and Claudia always gave her evasive replies. Especially lately, when Amy suggested Steve would be a good candidate.

"Um, I suppose I am settled. I like my job and my home here. I . . . I don't really think much about marrying again." Which wasn't entirely true, but Claudia didn't think of it as a lie, either. And standing next to Steve, so tall and manly, the warm sense of security she felt made her realize that having a man in her life again would not be such a bad idea. But marriage—well, that would really change her solo lifestyle.

Steve swallowed and nodded. "I'm glad you're happy."

"What about you?" she asked. "Would you like to remarry?"

He hesitated, then shrugged in a nonchalant way. "I guess I have about the same outlook as you do."

At that moment a voice could be heard from the guest room. "Smart bird. Smart bird. Tom? Tom? You listening?"

Knickerbocker looked up at Claudia, mystified.

"That poor parrot. They're very intelligent, you know. I've heard that African Greys not only talk, but they understand what they're saying. He must really miss Tom." Claudia took Steve's arm. "Let's go see how he's doing with Jasmine. The pizza will probably be here before too long. We can sit with him until then."

Steve smiled at her. "Sounds like a plan."

#

The next day Claudia had lunch with Amy at the Bumblebee Café. While cutting into her bratwurst, on a plate also heaped with dumplings and sauerkraut, Amy prompted Claudia to continue.

"So what happened after you had the pizza? Did Steve hang around?"

"A while." Claudia speared a shrimp from her salad with her fork. "I had a half-done jigsaw puzzle out on my dining room table. We worked on that for maybe forty-five minutes. He needed to be at the station early in the morning, so he said goodbye, and left.

"He didn't make a pass, try to kiss you or anything?" Amy sounded disappointed.

"No," Claudia answered, drawing out the word. "I didn't expect him to. We're just friends." Though Steve's friendly hug in the guest room still played in her mind. And his masculine presence had elevated her senses in a way she hadn't felt for years.

"Well, that's something else you both have in common," Amy quipped, "besides being widowed and Irish. You're both slow movers."

Claudia made an effort to change the subject. If she had some budding feelings for Steve, she wasn't ready to discuss them with Amy. Or Amy would start planning for a wedding!

96

"So I need to get my hair cut. Do you know of a good hairdresser? Mine is going on maternity leave. I have a feeling once her baby is born, she might not come back to the salon, at least for a while."

"My sister quit the hair business when she had her kids," Amy said. "She cuts mine as a favor. I wouldn't know who to recommend."

"I just remembered," Claudia said, sitting up straighter. "Ethel Radek mentioned she went to a new place. They gave her a nice cut."

"Might as well give it a try. Have they figured out who murdered her husband?"

"No, but Steve said the autopsy showed that the murder weapon was probably a pair of scissors," Claudia said. "The police noticed that there were sewing materials and a machine out. Makes sense. I recall Ethel mentioning a few years ago that she sewed her own clothes. So Steve asked Ethel if she used long scissors to cut cloth, and she said she did. But the scissors are missing, and there's no other weapon that's been found."

"Could Ethel have done it?" Amy asked.

"Oh, no. She told the police she was playing bingo at the Wheaton senior center, and her story was confirmed. Steve and I went there, and he showed the supervisor a photo of Ethel."

Amy leaned over her bratwurst toward Claudia. "Wait a minute. You went with Steve on the investigation?"

"He thought since I knew Ethel, I might be of help."

Amy smiled as she cut another piece of sausage. "He may be a slow mover, or maybe he's just matching your pace. Looks like he has a strategy anyway."

"What?"

"Never mind. Eat your salad," Amy said with impatience. "And when you go to the salon, ask the hairdresser for a new style. You have beautiful hair—do something with it."

Claudia's head went back. "I like it long and straight. It's easy to put in a ponytail to stuff under my surgical cap."

Amy sighed. "So darn practical. I'm sure all the kitty cats appreciate it."

Despite feeling a little piqued, Claudia had to laugh at Amy's jibe. "I'm temporarily taking care of Tom's parrot and Ethel's cat. Last night the parrot started preening my hair. So it's not just kitty cats who appreciate it."

Amy smiled. "Yeah, okay. I give up."

#

That evening, Claudia phoned Ethel. "Jasmine is fine. She's eating well and looked happy to be with Hal again. Hal seems to be adjusting okay."

"I'm so glad," Ethel said. "It's a great comfort to me to know you're taking good care of Jasmine. And Hal, too."

"By the way, when you brought Jasmine to the clinic, remember I complimented you on your

98

haircut? You said you'd gone to a new salon. Would you give me the name of the place?"

"Oh, sure. It's in Wheaton. The Cut N Snip Salon. Ask for Jennifer. She's great."

"Thanks," Claudia said, writing down the recommendation. After more chit-chat, she said goodbye. As she looked at the note she'd written, she wondered why Ethel liked to go to Wheaton, not only for bingo, but for a haircut, too.

Chapter 5: The Cut N Snip Salon

The Cut N Snip Salon had a springtime décor that came as a surprise when stepping out of the light snow falling outside. The waiting area had wicker furniture with floral seat cushions. A vase holding artificial peonies stood on a long wicker table that featured an assortment of the current pop culture and hairstyle magazines.

Jennifer Wilson, the young, auburn-haired and slightly hyper stylist Ethel recommended, welcomed Claudia to her station, one of a dozen or so in the salon. Wearing a beautiful up-do and a zebra patterned apron, Jennifer fingered Claudia's long blond locks. "Your hair has nice body and texture. You just want the ends trimmed?"

Claudia hesitated, Amy's words turning in her mind. "I guess so. Unless you have some suggestion." She explained that she needed to easily hide it under her surgical cap.

"I can show you how to arrange it into a French braid—a high, thick braid at the back. It's pretty and it would give you a different look."

"Okay," Claudia agreed.

She followed Jennifer to a sink and got her hair washed, then sat in the revolving chair in front of a tall mirror at Jennifer's station.

As Jennifer began snipping ends, she chatted. "You said Ethel recommended me. She came in for the first time last week. Glad she liked me."

"Yes, I complimented her on her new cut." Claudia didn't know if Jennifer had heard about Tom Radek's murder, and decided not to mention it.

Jennifer went on talking. "Do you know Ethel's twin sister? She's been coming here for about a year now."

Claudia sat unblinking, processing what Jennifer said. "Ethel has a twin?"

"Eleanor Mason. She's very sweet. More shy and soft-spoken than Ethel. But they look so much alike. Identical not fraternal."

"Ethel has a twin," Claudia repeated, letting it sink in. "I never knew that. Where does she live?"

"Here in Wheaton, I think. I've run into her at the grocery up the street. She uses a walker. Said she was in a terrible car accident many years ago and it left her with a bad back." Jennifer shook her head as she continued to cut Claudia's hair. "A sad thing to happen to such a nice lady. She lives alone. Never married."

Thoughts swirled in Claudia's mind. When Jennifer was finished blowing dry and braiding her hair, Claudia wrote her a check. She hurried to her car, where she pulled out her cell phone.

"Steve, it's Claudia." In a rush, she told him what she'd just learned about Ethel's twin. "Eleanor uses a walker. Remember the woman at the funeral with the hat and scarf covering her face? And when

101

Tom and Ethel were at the clinic the day he was murdered, I heard him say to Ethel that he wanted to go help out Eleanor because she has a bad back."

"I wonder if Eleanor plays bingo," Steve said.

"That thought occurred to me, but I don't want to believe it," Claudia replied.

"How did you learn about Eleanor?"

"I went to a hair salon Ethel told me about. The stylist does Eleanor's hair, too."

"Good sleuthing," Steve said.

"Not really. All I came for was a haircut."

"Going home? Today's your afternoon off, right?"

"Yes."

"I'll find out where Eleanor lives and come by and pick you up."

She remembered Amy being surprised that Steve asked her to come along on his investigation. "Is it okay with the police department for me to accompany you when you do your interviews?"

"You've been a great help," he said, his tone sincere. "You knew Tom. You're friendly with Ethel. And you have a gentle and kind manner. You got Mia to tell us what was troubling her. I think you'll be equally good at talking to Ethel's sister. Nobody feels comfortable around a police detective. You're my biggest asset on this case."

Claudia swallowed, feeling affirmed and flattered that Steve thought so highly of her. "Well, okay then. Thank you. See you soon." She slipped her phone into her pants pocket and nervously drove home, telling herself not to jump to conclusions about Ethel or the murder.

When she got home, she saw Knickerbocker stretched out in the sun on the back of the couch by the front window. She gave him a gentle stroke, then walked to the guest room. Opening the door, she found Jasmine on the bed, curled up. The cat raised her head as Claudia entered. Hal was inside his cage eating from the small dish of parrot food. She'd left the door to the cage open, so he could be free.

Hal looked at her sideways. "Hello. Smart bird. Smart bird."

"Yes, you are," Claudia told him. And then on a hunch, remembering Tom took the bird with him everywhere, she said, "Eleanor. Eleanor."

"Shoulda married you," Hal said. "Wrong sister. Shoulda married you."

Chapter 6: Eleanor

As Steve drove his unmarked police car to Wheaton, Claudia told him what the parrot said when she recited Eleanor's name.

"'Shoulda married you,'" Steve repeated. "Hmm. You suppose there was a love triangle going on between Tom and Ethel and Eleanor?"

"I never would have guessed it." Claudia thought a moment. "Though when I heard Tom say he wanted to help Eleanor, Ethel remarked in a snarky tone that Eleanor was clever at coming up with stuff for him to do." Claudia sighed. "But I don't know if we should read too much into that. Tom and Ethel have been bringing Jasmine to the clinic for years. Ethel's a little high-strung and emotional. She'd get annoyed that Tom didn't always listen to her. She talks so much, I couldn't blame him for tuning her out. But they seemed to get along. At the funeral the priest said they'd been married for forty-four years."

"How long ago did Tom acquire Hal?" Steve asked.

Claudia contemplated. "Not sure. A couple of years ago? That's about when Tom started coming in with the parrot."

"So where would Hal have picked up those phrases?'"

"When he visited Eleanor." Claudia felt troubled at the thought.

"If we're lucky, we'll soon find out." Steve pulled up in front of a small, wood-frame house painted a pale avocado green. The house stood on a street lined with similar modest homes.

Hardened snow crunched under their feet as Steve and Claudia walked up the unshoveled sidewalk that led to the front door. Steve rang the bell.

In half-a-minute or so, a woman who looked very much like Ethel, except that she was leaning on a walker which prevented her from fully opening the door, peered out at them. "I don't make donations, if that's what you're looking for."

Steve quickly pulled out his badge. "Detective Steve O'Rourke, Briarwood police. You're Eleanor Mason, correct?"

Her hazel eyes widened. "Have I done something wrong? I know I didn't come to a full stop at that stop sign the other day. My car was sliding on the ice."

"No, no, you're not in trouble," Steve assured her. "I'm investigating Tom Radek's death. This is Claudia Bailey. She knew Tom. Just need to ask you a few questions."

"Oh." Eleanor bowed her head and leaned forward, putting all her weight on the walker. "Poor Tom. What an awful thing to happen. He was such a good man."

"Would you mind if we come in for a few minutes?" Steve asked politely.

The grey-haired lady looked up. "Of course. Of course. I'm sorry. Come in, please." She backed up her walker to let them enter.

Stamping snow off her boots on the doormat before going in, Claudia was struck by the difference in Eleanor's self-effacing manner and soft-spoken voice compared to her sister's. Perhaps Eleanor's bad car accident years ago had humbled her nature. Or maybe, though look-alikes, the twins had always been different in personality. The old nature or nurture question.

Eleanor invited them to sit on her living room couch, upholstered in a rust brown color. Sunlight streamed in through the lace-trimmed curtains pulled back from the front window. Pushing aside her walker, she sat in an easy chair facing them. A low, round coffee table with crossword puzzle books stood between the sofa and chair.

"How did you first meet Tom?" Steve asked.

The lady smiled. "Why, in high school. I had a big crush on him. We went steady for about six months. But then Ethel started to like him, too. She set her cap for him, and after high school he married her."

Claudia glanced at Steve. His eyes met hers indicating they were both remembering what the parrot said.

"Did you mind that he married your sister?" Claudia asked in a between-us-girls manner.

"Well, at the time I thought that if he preferred Ethel, I should give way. I wanted him to be happy. Ethel was more outgoing than me, so I knew it was natural for him to be drawn to her."

Steve gave Claudia a slight nod to urge her to continue.

"I know Tom used to come over to help you around the house," Claudia said.

"Oh, yes, he was the kindest man." Eleanor's eyes filled with tears. "I'm going to miss him terribly." She took a handkerchief out of the sleeve of her pink cardigan sweater and dabbed away the wetness.

"Did you ever wish he hadn't married your sister?" Claudia carefully asked. "Did he ever say he wished he'd married you?"

Eleanor stared at Claudia. "But . . . how did you know? Did Tom confide in you?"

"No. This will sound odd. His parrot, which I'm taking care of at the moment, said, 'Shoulda married you,' and 'Wrong sister.' Did he bring Hal with him when he came here to help out?"

Eleanor blinked hard and looked wistful. "He started bringing Hal along a couple of years ago. You're right. Before he would leave after a visit, he'd kiss me on the forehead and say, 'I should of married you, Eleanor.' Or he'd say, 'I married the wrong sister.' The parrot started imitating him."

"That must have been difficult for you to hear," Claudia said, feeling sad for the woman.

Eleanor tilted her head. "What could we do after all these years? Ethel wouldn't let him go without a fight, and I didn't want to take him away from her. I'm an invalid. He was better off with her. But it *was* sad the day he and I figured out what a misunderstanding there had been, all those years ago."

"A misunderstanding?" Steve said.

"Tom confided something to me a few weeks ago," Eleanor told them. She chewed her lip a moment, then continued. "He said that, back in high school, my sister had told him I only went out with him because I felt sorry for him. You see, in those days Tom was a math whiz, not especially handsome and maybe a little awkward. Some called him a nerd." Eleanor shook her head and sighed. "Well, I assured Tom that was never true at all. Tom was my first and only love. But I honestly thought Tom preferred my sister. So I let him go, wanting him to have what I thought he wanted. Tom said he wished he hadn't believed what Ethel told him years ago, because he *did* like me better."

"Your sister stole him away," Claudia said with astonishment.

"Yes, she did." Eleanor pressed her lips together, as if suppressing a spark of anger. She took in another long breath and slowly let it out. "After we realized Ethel had broken us up long ago, Tom started saying he'd married the wrong sister. Ethel can be overbearing and demanding. I guess she got on his nerves. Sometimes I wondered if he visited me to have a respite from her."

"What's your relationship with Ethel like?" Claudia asked out of curiosity.

"Oh . . . on again, off again," Eleanor replied in an uneasy way. "We have that twin bond, you know. It's a real thing. I love her. But sometimes . . . . And she did tell Tom that lie." She threw up her hands. "Well, what's past is past. I had to forgive her. She loved Tom, too. She even worked to put him through college."

Steve paused and then looked directly at Eleanor. "I need to ask you something. Just a routine question for our investigation."

Eleanor looked back at him expectantly. "Okay."

"Do you play bingo at the Wheaton senior center on Mondays twice a month?"

"Yes, I do. Wouldn't miss it. Why?"

"Does your sister know you play bingo there regularly?" Steve asked.

"I think I've mentioned it to her. Been going there for years. Why?"

Steve seemed to ignore her *why* questions. "Were you there the day Tom was murdered?"

"Well . . . ," Eleanor paused, lifting her hand to her cheek. "Oh, yes, it was that evening after bingo that I heard about it on the radio. I tried to call Ethel, but she wasn't home. She's like me, won't be bothered with those stupid smart phones. The answering machine came on, but I was in such

109

shock I couldn't think what message to leave. I hung up."

"Have you been in contact with Ethel since?" Steve asked.

"Late that night she called from the hotel," Eleanor said. "She was very upset. Finding him dead, stabbed like that, who wouldn't be? I went to the funeral of course, but didn't have much chance to talk to her. I'm kind of waiting until she's ready to have a heart-to-heart. I'm still recovering myself, so I understand. Who could have done such a thing? Do you know who murdered Tom?"

"We're still investigating," Steve said. "Haven't found the murder weapon yet."

"I hope you do," Eleanor said. "It might have fingerprints, right?"

"Right." Steve smiled. "Thank you. What you've told us may be helpful."

A look of guilt crossed Eleanor's face. "Please don't let my sister know that I told you about her fib years ago. She can fly into a fury sometimes, and I don't want her mad at me. We were all so young then. With Tom gone, I don't want that to come between us."

"I'll keep that in mind," Steve said.

After bidding Eleanor goodbye, Steve and Claudia got back into the unmarked Charger.

Claudia asked, "You think Hal repeated 'Shoulda married you' at home, and Ethel heard him? But I can't believe she'd kill her husband over something a parrot said."

"We know Ethel's alibi about playing bingo was a lie," Steve replied. "She probably remembered Eleanor would be at the Wheaton senior center at that time, and she could claim it was her. Apparently it wasn't well-known that Ethel had a twin."

"But I just can't believe Ethel could be capable of murder. Maybe she only said she was at bingo because she knew that, being the spouse, she'd be the prime suspect." Claudia looked at Steve. "What about Greg Owen, Tom's business partner? Mia thought he had a motive and a fiery temper, too."

"Owen was arrested today for embezzlement," Steve informed her. "We're still looking into his whereabouts at the time of the murder."

"It must have been him," Claudia said with confidence. "Would a woman who sewed her own clothes and loved her cat so dearly murder her husband of forty-four years?"

Steve glanced at her, his eyes full of caring patience. "You'd be surprised. We need to talk to Ethel again."

"Now?"

"No time like the present," Steve said. "By the way, your hair looks very nice."

"Think so? The hairstylist braided it."

"Looks poetic. You could be the graceful, sweet heroine in a Jane Austen movie."

"Thank you," Claudia replied, surprised and pleased at such a romantic compliment. How many men would say something so charming?

She realized she had to face an undeniable truth: Steve was a keeper.

Chapter 7: Somebody at the Door

They drove to the Briarwood Arms, but unfortunately Steve and Claudia found that Ethel was not there. The woman behind the reception desk said she saw Ethel leave about an hour before.

"I'll take you home then," Steve told Claudia. "I've got some things to catch up on at the station."

He dropped her off, saying he'd see her later. Claudia unlocked her front door to find Knickerbocker sitting just inside the threshold looking up at her with his emerald eyes, as if to say, *Where have you been?*

"Hi, sweetie." She picked up the big, fluffy Maine Coon to give him a cuddle. He seemed perfectly at home now, as if he no longer remembered his former house. Claudia reminded herself to write to Sue Ember and tell her Knickerbocker was doing well.

After taking off her wool overcoat, she played with the cat, dangling his favorite ribbon in front of him. But he soon got bored in his feline way and jumped up on the couch, no doubt for another snooze. Somehow reluctant to check on Jasmine and Hal in the guest room, Claudia reached for her jump rope coiled by the bookcase, telling herself some exercise might calm her apprehensive feelings about Ethel.

She was just breaking into a sweat when her phone rang. Tossing the jump rope onto an easy chair, she picked up her cell phone. "Hello."

"Claudia? It's Steve."

"Hi." At that moment, her bell rang. "Oh, somebody's at the door. Can you wait?"

"Sure."

"Hold on, I'll be quick."

She opened the door to find Ethel standing there. Claudia instantly made an effort to disguise her shock. "Ethel," she said in a robust voice, still holding the cell phone, hoping Steve could overhear. She forced a smile. "I tried to visit you at the hotel a little while ago."

"I went shopping to buy some clothes," Ethel began in her talkative manner. "Didn't have a chance to take much out of my closets, and I don't want to go to the house. I was nearby and thought I'd stop and ask if I could visit Jasmine. Just for a few minutes, that's all. Today is your afternoon off, isn't it? The clinic closes early?"

"Yes," Claudia said, deeply uneasy about letting her in. "Jasmine is fine. I'm afraid it's not a good time." She held up the phone. "I'm on an important call."

"Oh, you just go ahead and talk," Ethel said, stepping in front of Claudia into the living room as Knickerbocker ran into the dining room. "I'll only be a minute. Just want to see my baby. Where is she?" Ethel unbuttoned her faux-fur collared overcoat and draped it over an easy chair.

"I've got her in my guest room." Claudia was at a loss as to how to get rid of the woman.

Ethel chuckled, straightening her red sweater over her wool pants. "Of course. She *is* your guest. I knew you would take excellent care of her until I'm settled somewhere. You're very kind, and I so appreciate it."

As Ethel crossed the living room, looking around, Claudia held the cell phone to her ear with trembling fingers and softly said, "Did you hear?"

"On my way. Don't go near her!" She heard the click as Steve ended the call.

"Where did you say?" Ethel asked, looking confused.

"The guest room's this way." Claudia started heading in that direction, trying to sound friendly, yet keeping several feet of distance between them. Her heart was beating fast with anxiety. "Have you started looking at apartments or condos?"

"I looked at a couple of condos, but they didn't suit me."

Claudia carefully opened the door of the guest room and peeked in. She saw Jasmine curled up on the bed, but couldn't spot where Hal was. She'd been leaving his cage open and he wasn't in it.

"She's on the bed. Go on in." She opened the door fully so Ethel could enter. Claudia stayed near the door.

Jasmine sat up and walked across the bed toward Ethel, who was saying, "There's my Jasmine. There's my pretty girl."

115

Claudia watched them, relaxing a little, until all at once she saw a movement from the corner of her eye. She looked up, and at the top of a bookcase, Hal was flapping his wings in agitation.

"Wrong Sister. Wrong Sister. No don't!" The parrot suddenly took off and hurled itself at Ethel. It dive bombed her hair, digging its claws into her scalp, screeching.

"Stop! Get away!" Ethel waved her hands around her head trying to fend the bird off.

Claudia watched in horror. "You did it, didn't you?" she said, her voice breathless.

"Let me out of here!" Ethel screamed. She turned and ran into the living room, but the bird came after her.

"No don't!" the bird screeched, landing on her shoulder, then biting her earlobe, drawing blood.

As Ethel headed to the front door, Claudia caught up to her, extended her foot and tripped the older woman. Ethel fell to the floor face down, the bird still biting and sinking its claws into her neck and head. Though Claudia wanted to get the angry parrot away from her, she knew it was more important to keep Ethel from escaping. Or from trying to murder *her*. She grabbed her jump rope off the nearby chair and tied Ethel's hands behind her back with one end of the rope.

"I'm calling the police," Claudia told her as she pulled her cell phone from her pants pocket.

"No!" Ethel continued to turn her head this way and that to dodge the enraged parrot.

116

"You killed Tom!" Claudia exclaimed as she dialed 911.

"He deserved it!" Ethel screamed, lifting her head off the carpet. "Get this bird off of me, for pity's sake!"

All at once the front door opened and Steve walked in. He took one look at Ethel tied up and struggling against the parrot. "Good work, Claudia."

"I called 911," Claudia told him, showing him her phone.

"I'll take it."

As he spoke to the emergency operator, Claudia hurried to her linen cupboard in the hall and grabbed a pillow case. She opened it up and took the crazed parrot by surprise, closing him up inside. Hal grew quiet, suddenly encased in darkness. Taking the captured bird to the guest room, she left him on the bed, still in the pillow case, figuring it would take a minute before he found his way out of it. Meanwhile, Jasmine hopped off the bed and ran out into the living room before Claudia could close the door on Hal. She followed as the Himalayan moved toward Ethel on the floor, sniffing at her and meowing.

Ethel turned her head to the cat. "Oh, Jasmine." She looked up at Steve. "I'm going to jail, aren't I?"

"Yes." He gave Claudia her phone, then crouched behind Ethel to handcuff her and remove the rope. "Squad car is on the way. We have evidence. Security cameras at an intersection in downtown Briarwood show your car and your license plate there at the time you claimed you were in Wheaton playing bingo. We know that was your twin sister. You murdered your husband, left, maybe changed out of bloody clothes, then came back later and called 911, pretending you'd discovered him dead."

"Security cameras?" Claudia said. "You didn't mention that."

"Got the report at the station a little while ago," he explained. "That's what I was calling to tell you."

"Why did you kill Tom?" Claudia asked Ethel.

Before she could answer, Steve informed her, "You have the right to remain silent. Anything you say can and will be used against you in a court of law. You have the right to have an attorney—"

"Oh, never mind all that," Ethel interrupted. "Can I sit up?"

Steve helped her shift to a sitting position on the floor, her handcuffed hands behind her. Claudia assumed Ethel would keep quiet.

"It's all that stinking bird's fault!" Ethel cried, her voice harsh.

"Shh, you shouldn't say anything," Claudia told her, kneeling next to her.

"What does it matter now?" Ethel argued, spots of blood in her hair and ear from Hal's attack. "I've lost everything. That awful parrot Tom took everywhere blabbed on him. He visited Eleanor after we left the clinic. When he came home the

118

bird squawked, "Wrong sister. Shoulda married you." She looked to Claudia for sympathy. "Well, how would you feel if you found out your husband wished he'd married your twin?"

"Devastated, I suppose," Claudia replied.

"I asked Tom if that's what he'd said to Eleanor. He wouldn't answer. I kept after him and he turned off his hearing aid! He did that a lot. I just got enraged and picked up my scissors. I held them up to scare him. Made him admit that he did prefer Eleanor."

Sirens and motorcycles could be heard outside drawing near, but Ethel continued her rant. "He said he was sick of me talking, always demanding attention, and that Eleanor was considerate and quiet. He claimed he could have a *real* conversation with her. That she knew how to listen. Ha! So I . . . I stabbed him. It just happened. I didn't mean to. But he was so disrespectful to *me*, who'd been his wife for forty-four years! Why, he cared more about that horrible parrot than me. I deserved better than that. Don't you think?"

Claudia leaned back on her heels and did not reply.

The front door opened and uniformed police came pouring in, five or six of them. Steve got up to talk to them.

Ethel began to look frightened. "I really will be taken to jail," she said to Claudia.

"Well . . . you did murder your husband. And tried to hide it with a phony alibi," Claudia told her. "Did you think you could get away with it?"

"I did . . . for a while." Ethel glanced at Jasmine who was staring at her with stark, round eyes. "Will you take my kitty?"

"Sure, of course I will." Claudia hesitated. "What about Hal?"

"Pluck him and cook him, for all I care." Ethel looked up at the police officers who were gathering around her. "Alright, alright, I won't put up a fight."

They lifted her to her feet and took her away. After they'd left, Steve helped Claudia get up from her kneeling position.

"I have to go to the station to book Ethel," Steve told her. "Did I hear you say you'd adopt her cat?"

Claudia spread her hands. "I couldn't say no." She turned to see that Jasmine and Knickerbocker, who had taken refuge in the dining room, had noticed each other. Knickerbocker growled at Jasmine and she hissed back. And then they ignored each other. "Well, maybe they'll get along. I hope Hal is okay."

She opened the door to the guest room, and Hal flew out. After a turn around the living room, he landed on Claudia's shoulder. "Smart bird."

"You going to keep him, too?" Steve asked.

She sighed. "I don't know. You think maybe Eleanor would take him?"

"Worth a try. Hal knows her."

Chapter 8: Life Won't Be the Same

The following Sunday turned out to be a clear, sunny day. After attending church and enjoying their usual brunch at The Old Mill restaurant, Steve suggested to Claudia that they go for a stroll down the graveled pathway that was once the railroad track of a commuter train to Chicago. The railroad had gone out of business decades ago, and local suburbs had removed the old tracks and turned the wide path into a miles long, tree-lined promenade.

As they walked, Steve caught her up on remaining elements of the Tom Radek murder case.

"We found the murder weapon in the neighbor's compost heap, where Ethel confessed she'd thrown the scissors as she fled the house. She'd shut the door on the parrot who was coming after her. She told us she changed outfits in her garage—she had some wash drying on the clothesline in there. She'd thrown her bloody clothes in someone's trash can before driving off. Garbage has been picked up, so we may never find those. But there's more than enough evidence, plus her confession, to convict her. Also, Greg Owen was at a car dealership buying a Mercedes at the time of the murder. But he'll be put away for embezzlement. Mia should be happy about that."

"It's all so sad," Claudia said. "Too bad Tom believed Ethel years ago when she told him her sister was going with him only because she felt sorry for him. If he'd married Eleanor, none of this would have happened."

"Marrying the right person is important," Steve agreed. He hesitated and glanced at Claudia. "Look, I've gathered that you're not in any hurry to marry again. But since we've been getting along well, seeing each other at church or on a case, you think maybe sometime we could go on a real date? I mean, like, dinner and a movie? Maybe a play in downtown Chicago? Or a Cubs game?"

Though pleased with his suggestion, Claudia suddenly felt shy and self-conscious. She pulled her wool overcoat closer to her chest. "It's been a long time since I've been on a date."

Steve bowed his head. "Me, too," he admitted. "We'll muddle through it together. Okay?"

Claudia smiled as she felt her breaths coming faster. "Sure. That would be nice."

He smiled back at her and nodded. "Great. So . . . you think I could say you're my girlfriend?"

Her eyes widened. "Um . . .all right."

"Terrific." He slipped his arm around her shoulders and they walked on quietly.

Her heart thumping, Claudia felt a little flabbergasted that now, all at once, she had a boyfriend. She'd have to get used to the idea before she told Amy or anyone else.

After several moments of silence between them, he asked, "So how are your two cats getting along?"

"Surprisingly well," she replied, catching her breath. "There was some spitting and paw swatting for a few days, but now they seem at peace. Their food bowls are next to each other, and they eat together with no problem. By the way, Eleanor did take Hal. She was happy to give him a home because she knew that was what Tom would have wanted."

"Good. So you're just a cat collector, for now anyway."

She laughed. "Hope I don't get involved in any more murders. I don't need any more cats. Not that I mind having Jasmine and Knickerbocker."

"I hope you do," he gently contradicted. "You're really good at getting people to talk. You were a great help on both our murder cases."

"I'd like to stick to being a veterinary technician, thank you very much," she told him archly. When he looked disappointed, she added, "And being your girlfriend."

Steve gave her a big grin. And then he took her in his arms and soundly kissed her.

Claudia's toes curled, and she felt dazed as he released her. He took her hand and they walked on together as a couple.

My life won't be the same anymore. The thought unsettled her. Still, as they ambled along

the tree-lined path on a sunny day, the future
suddenly seemed happier.

Novella III
THE CLAIRVOYANT CAT

Chapter 1: A Few Years Earlier

The small TV in the employees' break room at the Briarwood Cat Clinic was tuned to the local noontime news. Dressed in green cotton scrubs, Claudia Bailey had finished her lunch and was stitching a needlepoint canvas when Trudy Avery, the clinic's office manager, came in. A plump, pretty, fifty-something lady wearing a blue pantsuit, Trudy's short hair was an eye-catching shade of blonde.

"Busy morning, huh?" Trudy said as she took her homemade salad encased in a plastic container out of the refrigerator. She sat down at the small table across from Claudia.

Claudia nodded, looking up as she drew out a thread. "I always appreciate lunch hour." She couldn't help but gaze admiringly at Trudy's hair, shining in the room's ceiling lights. "I wonder if I should use a different shampoo or something. I'm blonde, but you're blondie-blonde."

Trudy chuckled. "Honey, this all comes from a bottle." She patted her bouncy locks. "Your hair is thick and long and beautiful. Leave it alone till you've got gray to hide. You'll save yourself a bundle, too."

Claudia smiled. "Thanks for the good advice. And the compliment."

"What's the picture you're needlepointing?"

Claudia held up the partly stitched square canvas stretched on a wood frame so Trudy could see.

"A cat," Trudy said, laughing. "Of course."

"When I saw this one at the needlepoint store, it reminded me of Taffy, the orange and white tabby my husband and I adopted. They're both gone now. I have a photo of my husband on the fireplace mantle. I thought it would be nice to have a pillow made from this canvas, in memory of Taffy."

"I remember she died last year. You live all alone now. Don't you want to adopt another cat?" Trudy gently asked.

"Maybe someday. I'm not ready yet," Claudia replied. "Don't know why, but I'm not."

"It's hard to let go when you lose loved ones," Trudy sympathized. She was quiet a moment, then pointed to the TV in back of Claudia. "Oh, look. They're talking about that cat that predicts Cubs games."

Claudia turned to see the sixteen-inch TV on the counter next to the small sink. Trudy got up to make the volume higher.

Ben Jordan, the handsome Chicago anchorman, sat at his desk in the studio with a photo of a white cat projected in back of him. "In a few minutes, we'll go to Briarwood City Hall where Wrigley the Clairvoyant Cat is scheduled to predict whether or not the Cubs will win the World Series."

"Oh, goody," Trudy said with excitement. "We're just in time to see it live."

Claudia drew her brows together. "You believe the cat can really predict who'll win?"

"Well, Wrigley has been right 82% of the time," Trudy said. "That's a pretty good record. I read it in the Briarwood Press."

Claudia politely shrugged. "I stand corrected." She wasn't sure a cat regularly put on display during baseball season, in front of a bunch of news photographers with flashing cameras waiting to see which bowl the cat would eat from, made a happy life for a feline. But she kept her thoughts to herself.

On the TV, the young, dark-haired anchorman was presenting a brief retrospective of how Wrigley was becoming well-known in Chicagoland as a Cubs prognosticator.

"It all started three years ago. Mrs. Lydia Worthington brought the new kitten she'd adopted from the DuPage County Love-A-Cat Shelter to a charity event raising money to support the no-kill shelter."

As Jordan spoke, a photo came on the screen of a short-haired white kitten on a cloth-covered table with two small bowls of dry cat food placed before him. One bowl was marked *Cubs* and the other *Reds*.

"It was playoff season," the anchorman continued, "and in front of the curious audience, the kitten chose to eat out of the *Cubs* bowl. Lo and behold, the Cubs won! And that was just the beginning, as you'll see in this interview we taped yesterday with Mrs. Worthington."

A new scene appeared on the TV screen. A pleasant and cheerful-looking white-haired lady, probably in her late seventies, sat in a garden with a large willow tree behind her. On her lap she held a full-grown, blue-eyed white cat who made an attempt to jump onto the glass-topped wrought iron table in front of her, but she gently restrained the cat from doing so. Jordan sat at the table with her.

"Looks like they filmed this in Lydia's backyard," Trudy said. "She's quite wealthy, I think. Lives on Castleberry Lane in a stately, two-story brick mansion with white columns and balustrades. Colonial Revival architecture, I heard someone say."

"That's in the upscale part of Briarwood," Claudia agreed. "How do you know all this?"

128

"She had a charity event at her house that I attended last year. For homeless veterans. She's widowed. Supports a lot of charities. She's a lovely lady."

They both listened to the conversation on TV.

"What first gave you the idea to have your cat, a mere kitten at the time, become a prognosticator?" Jordan asked.

Mrs. Worthington's face grew animated with infectious humor as she spoke in a lilting voice. "Well, on a sports report—I think it was your station—they showed a clip of a cat in Russia that predicts their big soccer games. I'd just adopted Wrigley. Actually I'd named him Blue at first, because of his stunning blue peepers." She cupped the cat's face, so the camera could show his deep-hued eyes. "I was in charge of the fund raiser for the Love-A-Cat Shelter that year. So I thought it would be fun to try copying what they do in Russia, and see what would happen. I wasn't sure he'd eat out of either dish with everyone watching him so closely," she explained, laughing. "But he did, and he picked the Cubs' bowl and the next day they won. Everyone seemed to enjoy it so much, I brought him to other charity events. By the end of that season, local newspaper reporters were covering Wrigley's predictions—I'd decided to change his name to Wrigley. The next year you TV reporters started showing up."

"And this year, Briarwood City Hall has been hosting Wrigley's predictions," the anchorman added.

"Our mayor said Wrigley has put Briarwood on the map," Lydia said with a smile. "Our historic town has always been in the shadow of Wheaton, Oakbrook and Elmhurst. Not anymore. Especially not since Wrigley correctly predicted the Cubbies would beat the L. A. Dodgers to win the pennant this year."

Jordan leaned forward. "I hear you have a theory as to why Wrigley has such a good track record at foretelling whether the Cubs will win. Something about his blue eyes?"

Lydia drew in a breath. "Yes, indeed. Now don't be sad, but Wrigley is deaf. White cats with blue eyes often have a hereditary condition that makes them deaf. I've heard the statistic is 65 to 85 percent. That's probably why no one had adopted him at the cat shelter."

Trudy turned to Claudia. "Is that true?"

Claudia nodded. "It's called congenital sensorineural deafness."

"Aww," Trudy sighed, looking crestfallen.

"Deaf cats do okay if they have a caring owner and they're kept indoors," Claudia assured her.

Meanwhile on TV, Lydia was saying, "But you see, that's why Wrigley's a good prognosticator. His deafness allows him to concentrate more deeply and pick up vibes from the universe that other cats and we humans aren't aware of."

Claudia rolled her eyes.

"Thank you, Mrs. Worthington, for letting us interview you and Wrigley." Jordan stretched out his hand across the table. Instead of taking his hand, the lady playfully held out Wrigley's paw. He laughed and gently shook it.

The TV screen switched back to the newsroom. "And now I'm told that Wrigley is about to make his prediction for the World Series," Jordan said with enthusiasm. "Let's go to Briarwood City Hall."

Trudy and Claudia leaned toward their small television as the scene changed to a spacious room with marble pillars. An antique wood table with carved legs had been set up, covered with a black tablecloth. A crowd of photographers had gathered around, many of them preparing their equipment, focusing their cameras. News reporters at the ready with microphones and digital recorders were also present.

The mayor said a few words of welcome and introduced Lydia Worthington. The lady stepped forward wearing a white lace dress, while a young man in a suit and tie followed carrying a blue leather cat carrier.

At the table, Mrs. Worthington held up an unopened bag of dry cat food. "This is Wrigley's favorite, duck and green pea. His veterinarian recommended it especially. I'm opening it in front of everyone so you know his food hasn't been tampered with and both bowls will be exactly the same."

131

Trudy turned to Claudia. "I wonder which vet he goes to?"

"Don't know," Claudia said.

"Wish it was ours," Trudy murmured as they watched while Lydia opened the bag and poured an equal amount of food kernels into each small crystal glass bowl. One bowl had a sign beside it that read *Cubs* and the other had a sign marked *Indians*. Ribbons with the colors of each team streamed from underneath the glass dishes and draped over the edge of the table.

"Now Brent Davies, my very handsome nephew, will open up Wrigley's carrier." Lydia motioned to the auburn-haired young man who had followed her. Smiling, he placed the carrier on a carved oak bench that had been placed nearby, zipped open the top flap and lifted out the white cat. He brought Wrigley, who appeared quite docile and did not squirm or put up a fight, to his aunt. She gathered the big feline in her arms and carried him to the table, as cameras began to flash. Lydia seemed to take care to place the cat in the middle of the table, equidistant between each bowl, which were placed about three feet apart. Then she let him go.

Trudy braced her hand against her nose. "Gosh, isn't this exciting?"

Claudia had to admit, it was quite a scene to watch.

Wrigley sniffed the dish marked *Cubs*, then walked over to the *Indians* bowl.

132

"Oh, no," Trudy whispered. "Go back, go back."

Wrigley hesitated, sat on his haunches for a moment, then walked over to the *Cubs* bowl again. He carefully sniffed the food—and began eating. Cameras flashed like crazy and people in the room began cheering.

Trudy jumped up from her chair, clapping and yelling, "Yay!"

Claudia grinned. "I hope he's right. My husband would have been thrilled to see that curse ended," she said, remembering how much Peter loved the Cubs.

Trudy turned to her, still excited. "That's right! It would break the curse if the Cubbies win."

Claudia tried to recall Peter's explanation of why the jinx came about. She wasn't all that much of a sports fan. Puzzled, she looked at Trudy. "What's the curse again? Something about a goat?"

Trudy seemed happy for the chance to repeat the tale. "It was in 1945. Game four of the World Series. The owner of the Billy Goat Tavern—it's still there at Wrigley Field, you know—wanted to bring his pet goat into the ballpark to watch the Cubs play. He took the goat with him everywhere. But fans in the bleachers complained the goat was too smelly, and he was asked to leave. He became outraged and yelled a curse against the Cubs as he left. It's said he also sent a telegram to the team owner, Mr. Wrigley himself, saying the Cubs would lose that World Series and would never win another. Because they'd insulted his goat."

"And they lost that game?"

"Oh, yeah," Trudy assured her. "And they've never won a World Series since."

On the TV, the commotion of flashing cameras and cheers at the Briarwood City Hall had calmed. A reporter from the TV station they were watching approached Lydia who was cuddling her cat.

Trudy grew silent, listening intently. Claudia leaned forward out of curiosity.

"You've got quite a popular puss there, Mrs. Worthington," the news reporter said, holding a microphone. He extended the mic toward the beaming white-haired lady.

"Oh, and don't I know it! I'm thinking of changing my will and leaving my estate to Wrigley," she said in a lighthearted tone.

The reporter looked surprised. "Really?"

"He's a special kitty. I don't have children or grandchildren. Wrigley is my baby, and I want to be sure he'll be taken care of, for the sake of his fans. And the Cubs."

"What about your handsome nephew?" The reporter gestured to Brent who had approached her, holding out his hands to take the cat.

"Brent is a clever, capable fellow," she said with pride as she carefully gave Wrigley to him. "He'll do very well."

The camera focused on Brent's expression. The thin, well-dressed young man's finely chiseled features appeared stoic. The reporter stuck the microphone in his face. Brent smiled, raised his dark eyebrows and simply said, "That's my Aunt Lydia."

The reporter turned to the camera. "You heard it here first," he said jokingly. "Back to you in the studio. Ben?"

Ben Jordan began reporting other news. Trudy turned down the volume on the TV as Mary Anne, the clinic's ponytailed, twenty-something receptionist came in for her lunch break. Trudy quickly told her that they'd just watched Wrigley predict the Cubs would win the Series.

"Great!" Mary Ann replied.

"Wrigley may be a wealthy cat someday," Trudy quipped as she and Claudia walked out together to go back to work.

"Amazing," Claudia agreed with humor.

Chapter 2: Present Day

On a hot afternoon at the end of summer, Claudia was happy to be indoors enjoying air conditioning. She stood behind the cat clinic's reception counter checking the schedule for the remainder of the day. Trudy sat nearby working at a computer. Dr. Chandler was in one of the treatment rooms examining an elderly calico as the cat's owner watched. Claudia wondered if the veterinarian would need her to draw blood or get a urine sample.

All at once, the clinic's glass entrance door burst open. Abigail Pressley and her young son Joey hurried in as if on a mission. Claudia looked up with surprise. None of Abigail's cats were on the schedule for a check-up or treatment. She heard a loud, agitated meow and saw that the young mom with short brown hair was holding a pet carrier.

"Hi, Mrs. Pressley," Claudia greeted her. "Is one of your cats sick?"

"No, but Joey was outside playing and he saw this injured cat." She lifted up the carrier so Claudia could see through its screened door. "We don't know who the cat belongs to. Its paws seem to have dried blood on them, there's blood around its mouth, and the poor thing looks exhausted. It must have been in some kind of fight or accident. When Joey heard it meowing, he discovered it under a parked car. He told me, and we managed to coax the cat out. It's almost like he—I think it's a male—was looking for help. He was all dirty with motor oil, too."

"He looked really scared," Joey, a towheaded boy of ten or eleven, told Claudia, concern in his young eyes. "I tried to give him some cat food, but he wouldn't eat."

"I'm willing to pay for his treatment," Abigail said, "but if he's a stray and no one claims him, I can't adopt him. We already have the three cats and two dogs."

"I understand." Claudia walked up to her and bent to peer more closely into the carrier. She saw blood and dirt on the feline's face, its blue eyes looking wide and frightened. And the cat was panting, a clear sign of stress. "We can scan to see if he has a microchip. If he does, that would lead us to his owner." She straightened up and spoke to Joey. "You did a very good deed," she told the boy. She turned to Abigail. "That's very generous of you to pay for his treatment."

Trudy came out from behind the counter. "We'll give you our good Samaritan discount. Kindness to animals should be rewarded."

"Thank you," Abigail said with appreciation in her voice. "So then, we'll leave him with you. I'll pick up the carrier later. Joey and I would like to know if the cat will be okay."

"We'll let you know," Claudia assured her as she took the carrier from Abigail.

Claudia brought the cat into the treatment room, set the carrier on an exam table and unlatched its door. The cat was still breathing through its mouth, not at all normal for a healthy feline. She checked the clinic's plug-in pheromone diffuser, which put out a scent that was calming to cats. The small bottle was full of fluid and didn't need replacing. She talked softly to the cat, who looked almost petrified with fear.

"You're safe here. We'll take good care of you." She extended her hand so the cat could smell her. When that went well, she gently stroked his dirty forehead, noticing the dried blood around its mouth. She wondered if the cat had a mouth injury or if he'd bitten someone in self-defense. The paws were also caked in dried blood. She could see what appeared to be a blood splatter on the cat's shoulder, which reminded her of the splatter on Hal the parrot's wing when Tom Radek had been murdered.

"Let's see if we can find out who you belong to." She picked up the white microchip scanner and let the cat smell it before extending it into the cage and over his back. Microchips were usually placed between a pet's shoulder blades. Sure enough the scanner beeped, indicating a chip had been detected. She looked at the readout on the scanner and wrote down the number, then hurried to the front desk to ask Trudy to look it up on the appropriate website.

As Claudia returned to the treatment room, she found the cat hesitantly creeping out of the carrier.

She quickly picked up a bag of treats and offered him a salmon flavored kernel. The cat sniffed and then ate it.

"Good kitty," she said soothingly, and gave him another treat.

Perhaps the pheromone scent was working, or maybe the cat just liked her gentle manner. In any case she needed to start her TPR check—temperature, pulse, and respiration. He'd stopped panting, so that was a good sign. To take the cat's pulse, she pressed her first two fingers against the inside of his upper hind leg, where the large femoral artery was located. The cat loudly meowed and began to squirm away. Fortunately, Dr. Chandler came in just then and deftly prevented the cat from jumping off the exam table. The grandfatherly, white-haired veterinarian held the cat still while Claudia proceeded to count its pulse, timing fifteen seconds on her watch.

"So this is the injured stray? Trudy told me." Dr. Chandler let the cat go when Claudia finished taking its pulse. They both observed as it walked, limping on the left front leg, to the edge of the exam table. Again, the veterinarian kept the cat from jumping off.

"Pulse is 230," Claudia told him as she entered the number on a computer file she was creating.

"High, but normal." Dr. Chandler took the stethoscope that hung from his neck and used it to listen to the cat's heart and lungs. As he checked its eyes and ears, Claudia got out a thermometer and

139

applied a dab of lubrication. After he'd finished looking into the cat's mouth, Dr. Chandler held the feline still as she inserted the thermometer under the tail.

"See any wounds in the mouth?" she asked.

"No. We better X-ray his left front leg."

She withdrew the thermometer. "Temperature is normal."

Together they placed the cat on the X-ray machine, stretching him to get a good image of the front leg. Once more the wary feline tried to get away, this time with a loud meow, but Claudia stroked his forehead again which seemed to calm him.

"He likes you," Dr. Chandler said with a smile. "But then they all do." Checking the X-ray images, the vet said, "No broken bones. Must be a soft tissue injury."

"A pulled muscle?" Claudia suggested. "If he got into a cat fight it would explain the blood on the mouth. But there's what looks like dried blood on all his paws, too. And some on his shoulder."

Dr. Chandler grabbed a white paper towel and wet it at the nearby sink. "Let's see if there's any injury." He took the cat's right front paw and began wiping off the dried blood and the dirt. "Looks like car grease. He's pretty filthy all over. Trudy said he was found hiding under a car."

"He may have crawled up into it to hide." Claudia felt sorry for the stressed feline.

The veterinarian closely examined the paw he'd wiped almost clean. "I don't see any injury. It's like he stepped in blood."

"I wonder if it's human," Claudia said with a worried sigh. "I think I should call Steve O'Rourke and ask if there's been anyone wounded at a place where a cat went missing."

"Your good-looking detective beau?" Dr. Chandler teased with a knowing wink.

Though her co-workers at the clinic seemed happy for Claudia that she had a man in her life again, and they'd all met Steve on several occasions, she still felt self-conscious about having a boyfriend. She wasn't sure why. She and Steve had been a couple for nearly six months now.

"Hal the parrot had a blood splatter the police needed to check when they investigated Tom Radek's murder," she said, ignoring the wink. "Let's hope this isn't a similar situation, but—"

"Better call him," the veterinarian agreed. "This cat looks basically healthy. We can wait on giving him a bath."

"He ate the treats I gave him," Claudia said as she found her smart phone in her tunic pocket.

"A good sign," Dr. Chandler said as Claudia speed-dialed Steve's number.

The phone rang twice. "O'Rourke." His tone was quick, all business.

"Steve, it's me."

"Hello, me." His low voice suddenly turned warm and upbeat.

141

She chuckled. "I'm at the clinic and we're treating a stray someone found. The cat seems traumatized and has blood on its paws and mouth. But no wounds. I was wondering—"

"Is it a white cat with blue eyes?" Steve interrupted.

"Well, he's covered with motor oil from hiding under a car, but, yes, he's probably all white. And he's got bright blue eyes."

"I'll send forensics to get samples of the blood."

"Oh," Claudia said with dismay. "Then there's been an altercation or . . . ."

"Possible murder. Mrs. Lydia Worthington. I'm at the scene now. Her living room is in disarray. She bled out on the floor from a head wound. Her cat Wrigley is missing and there are paw prints in the pool of blood."

Claudia's mouth dropped open. "You mean, this cat could be the one that predicts Cubs games?"

"Yup. I'll stop by to see him."

At that moment Trudy rushed in, jittery with excitement as she proclaimed, "The microchip says he belongs to Lydia Worthington. His name is Wrigley!"

"Did you hear that?" Claudia asked Steve, still holding the phone to her ear.

"Good to have that confirmation," Steve said. "I'll be there soon."

Feeling disconcerted as she turned off her phone, she told Trudy and Dr. Chandler in a hushed voice, "Mrs. Worthington is dead. May have been murdered. Forensics will be here to take samples from . . . from Wrigley."

"Oh, no." Trudy leaned weakly against the doorframe. "How awful."

Dr. Chandler gravely shook his head. "Dreadful. And if the cat saw her murdered, that would be a huge trauma." He stroked the feline's back in a slow, calming manner. "Maybe he needed to escape whoever did it."

Wrigley looked up at the veterinarian, then at Claudia, as if sensing the change in emotion in the humans around him. His blue eyes grew round with a lost aspect that broke Claudia's heart.

#

A female forensics expert from Briarwood Police came about twenty minutes later. Claudia helped keep Wrigley still while she scraped samples of the dried blood from the cat's paws, his shoulder, and from the fur around his mouth. When she was finished, Claudia let the cat rest in a three-by-five-foot cage partly covered with a towel so he would feel safe. Ordinarily she would take the cat to a quiet corner of the clinic, but she remembered that Wrigley was reportedly deaf. She clapped her hands sharply a few times, and the cat did not respond in any way. So she left him to rest in the treatment room until Steve showed up about forty-five minutes later.

"A neighbor of Mrs. Worthington heard the cat wailing violently," Steve, dressed in a suit and tie, told Claudia after she led him to the treatment room. Trudy left Mary Anne to take care of the reception counter and joined them. "The neighbor looked out the window," Steve continued, "and saw a thin man wearing a baseball hat and sunglasses run out of the house. Thought he saw reddish hair sticking out from under the cap, but wasn't sure. The suspect was trying to hold onto a white cat—the neighbor was sure it was Wrigley. The cat was frantically squirming to get out of the man's grasp. Neighbor thought he may have bitten the man's hand. Wrigley got away and took off in terror down the street. The suspect ran in another direction. The neighbor called 911."

"Who would kill an elderly lady and try to steal her cat?" Claudia asked, deeply troubled.

"A famous cat," Trudy pointed out. "She always told TV reporters that she was going to leave all her money to Wrigley."

Claudia nodded. "She'd say that with her nephew standing right next to her."

"Good point. I'd like to talk to him," Steve said. "Can I see the cat?" As Claudia pulled away the towel partly covering Wrigley's cage, Steve bent to observe the resting feline. "He does look like he's been through something awful."

Wrigley looked up at Steve suspiciously and moved to the back corner of the cage.

"If he was attacked by a guy, he might be afraid of men right now," Claudia explained. "Though he seemed to accept Dr. Chandler fairly well."

144

Steve straightened up. "Dr. Chandler has a calm, reassuring manner." He raised his eyebrows in a resigned expression. "We cops have an intimidating aura that maybe even animals sense."

Claudia touched his sleeve. "You have your reassuring moments, too."

He beamed at her. "Thank you."

"So what happens to Wrigley? We'll give him a bath and maybe a pain medication for his sore front leg. But then what?"

"Not sure," Steve said. "His home's a crime scene. His owner is dead."

"If Wrigley inherits Mrs. Worthington's fortune, then wouldn't her nephew want him?" Trudy asked. "Especially if he's the one who . . . ."

Claudia swallowed. "I'm willing to take Wrigley home with me until his future gets sorted out."

Steve's brown eyes darkened. "I don't like it. The perpetrator might still come after the cat."

"Nobody would know Wrigley was at my house," Claudia argued. "Only you know he's here, besides us. Has the public even heard he's missing?"

"They will," Steve said. "Word's gotten out that Mrs. Worthington's dead. Lots of police vehicles and satellite vans with reporters are blocking the street in front of her house. News media shot video of her covered body being carried out."

"Oh." Claudia looked down at the gray-tiled floor.

"The Commissioner wants me to do a press briefing," Steve said with a weary exhale. "Have to go back to her house now for that. Just wanted to see Wrigley for myself first."

Trudy perked up. "Will we be able to watch you on TV?"

"Some stations may carry it live," Steve told her.

"The reporters will ask about Wrigley," Claudia said. "What will you tell them?"

"That he's safe at an undisclosed location."

"So, if it's undisclosed, why not my house?" Claudia said. "I feel bad for Wrigley. He really needs to be cared for and comforted."

Steve's eyes softened as he studied her. "Let me think about it." He glanced at his watch. "The press briefing is supposed to be at 4:30 and it's after 4:00 already." He slipped his arm around her shoulders, gave her a quick hug and left.

After he'd gone, Trudy looked at Claudia, eyes aglow. "Steve really cares about you. Are you going to tie the knot?"

"You sound like my friend Amy," Claudia replied with a touch of impatience. "We've been dating less than six months. No need for a knot yet."

"But you've known him longer than that. Didn't you sit with him at church before you started dating? You shouldn't let a great guy like him get away."

146

"What if I'm not sure I want to marry again?"

"Well, that would be too bad." Trudy shrugged. "But okay. None of my business."

Claudia did not reply and Trudy walked out, leaving Claudia to wonder why friends seemed eager for her to get hitched. What was wrong with a woman staying single—even if she did have an awesome boyfriend?

#

A half hour later, Trudy peeked in while Claudia was in one of the exam rooms finishing a TPR on a diabetic tuxedo cat while its owner watched.

"The news conference is on," Trudy whispered.

Dr. Chandler came up behind her with a little smile as Trudy stepped back. "You can both go watch. I'll take over here."

"Temperature is 101. Respiration looks normal. I didn't get the pulse yet," Claudia told the vet as she hurried out.

The women rushed to the break room where the small TV was already turned on. Steve was standing behind a cluster of microphones. Using the authoritative monotone he reserved for official police work, he informed the reporters gathered around exactly what he'd told Claudia and Trudy earlier, with some added details. Mrs. Worthington had received a mortal head wound in what appeared to be a violent struggle. The living room was in disarray, but there'd been no evidence of a forced break-in. Mrs. Worthington may have let the

147

murderer in. The perpetrator was still at large. The scant description was of a man with reddish-brown hair, about six feet tall, wearing a cap with a big brim pulled low, sunglasses, white T-shirt, sneakers and blue jeans. Helicopters still searched the neighborhood.

"What happened to Wrigley?" a male reporter asked.

"The cat is safe and apparently healthy," Steve told him.

"Where is he?" the reporter persisted.

"We are not disclosing the cat's location."

"If Wrigley escaped the perpetrator and ran away, who found him? And where?"

Steve shook his head. "I don't have that information."

After taking a few more questions, he ended the press briefing. A reporter from the TV station at the scene concluded his live update and handed the news coverage back to the anchorman in the studio.

"Steve did a masterful job," Trudy said.

"He's always in command when he's on duty," Claudia agreed, turning to leave the break room.

"I'll stay here and sort out what supplies we need to order," Trudy said, "and keep an eye on the TV in case there's any new news."

About twenty minutes later, Steve came back to the clinic. Claudia was near the reception counter preparing a medication Dr. Chandler prescribed for the tuxedo cat.

"Be with you in a minute," Claudia told Steve. "Have to finish instructions for this med." She smiled at the cat's owner, a stout, gray-haired man, who was patiently sitting on one of the benches with his cat by his side in a carrier. "Almost done," she told the client.

After giving the man the medication and explaining how to administer it, she held open the door while he left with his cat. "That's our last patient today," she told Steve.

"Good. So . . . you still want to look after . . . ?"

She nodded. "Is that okay with Briarwood Police?"

He shrugged. "My colleagues pointed out that you did a great job keeping the parrot. But I want to escort you home."

"Okay."

At that moment, Trudy rushed in from the rear of the clinic. "Claudia!" She spotted Steve. "Oh, good, you're here. On the news—" she said breathlessly, pointing toward the short hallway from which she'd come. "Abigail Pressley and Joey—"

All three of them hurried to the break room. Apparently hearing the commotion, Dr. Chandler came in, followed by Mary Anne.

They gathered around the TV as the same reporter at the murder scene was holding a microphone in front of Abigail.

"We had no idea the cat could be Wrigley until we saw the news on TV," she was telling him. "He

149

was all dirty and sorry-looking when my son found him."

The reporter shifted the mic to Joey, who looked eager to chime in. "He had bright blue eyes like Wrigley. But we didn't know Wrigley was missing, so we just thought it was a stray."

"Where is the cat now?" the reporter asked Abigail.

"We brought him to the Briarwood Cat Clinic. Claudia, their vet technician, assured us they'd look after him. It's an excellent clinic. We take our cats there."

"Great," Steve muttered with angry consternation as a cold clammy feeling swept down Claudia's face and neck. Steve turned to her. "Anyone can find your full name on the clinic's website. Grab Wrigley. Cover his carrier. We need to leave fast. Reporters will be here in minutes. Dr. Chandler, Trudy, I advise you to close up for the night, pronto."

Everyone seemed to jump as the clinic's phones began to ring.

"Nobody answer that!" Steve instructed as he took Claudia's arm and hurried her to the treatment room. There he helped her transfer Wrigley, who yowled in protest, out of the cage and into a carrier. They covered the carrier with towels and rushed outside. Steve's unmarked police car was parked not far from her Prius in the clinic's lot.

"I'll take him, okay?" Steve said. "If there's anyone following, I'll know what to do. I'll be right behind you. Go your usual way. Park your car in your garage and close the door."

"All right," Claudia said, her breaths growing short.

"Don't get shook." He squeezed her hand. "Just drive home like normal. Let's go."

Chapter 3: A Murderer Loose

Claudia drove home as normally as she could, her hands tightly gripping the wheel. Steve's car stayed right behind her. She used her remote to open her garage door, parked inside and closed the door. As she turned her house key in the lock, entered her kitchen and switched on the lights, she heard someone knocking at her back door.

"It's Steve," he called when she hesitated to open it.

She pushed aside the curtain on the door's window and saw it was indeed him.

As she let him in, she asked, "Where's Wrigley?"

"Right here." He reached back to pick up the covered carrier from her wood patio. "I parked around the corner. Didn't see anyone following us. I called for backup to guard your house."

"Thank you."

"In addition," he took a breath, "I'm spending the night with you."

"Oh." She felt a little startled. They may have been dating steadily for months, but he'd never stayed overnight.

"There's a murderer loose and you've got the cat he wanted. And you haven't had the security system installed that I recommended. Your name is on the clinic's website. You wouldn't be hard to find."

Chagrined, Claudia looked down at the floor. She felt she lived in a safe neighborhood, had never had any problem, so she'd been dragging her feet on following his advice. She didn't want to have to worry about a security code or unintentionally setting off an alarm.

Steve continued. "You need someone to guard you and Wrigley inside the house as well as outside."

She raised her head and nodded. "I see."

He lifted his right hand as if taking an oath. "I promise I'm not trying to barge in on you. You like your own space and I respect that. I'll be fine on the couch."

"No, no. You can have the guest room," she offered.

"Actually, it's better if I stay in the living room, where I can hear any unwanted activity. I'll probably stay awake all night."

"How's Wrigley?" She went up to the carrier Steve had set on the small, maple wood table, and pulled off the towels covering it. Wrigley looked through the screened door at her, his eyes wide with fright. He began to meow loudly.

"Shh, it's okay," she softly said as she opened the door to pet him. He seemed afraid to come out. He'd gotten somewhat used to the treatment room at the cat clinic, but now he was in yet another place unknown to him.

Suddenly Knickerbocker and Jasmine came into the kitchen, side by side, probably to investigate the meow of a strange cat.

"Oh, boy," she muttered and looked at Steve. "I'd better put Wrigley in the guest room by himself." She closed the door of the carrier and left the kitchen with Wrigley, followed by Knickerbocker and Jasmine who did not look happy about a feline intruder in their territory.

Claudia was getting Wrigley settled in the guest room with a bowl of water, some cat food, and a fresh litter pan, when Steve knocked on the door. She'd closed it to keep her two suspicious cats away from Wrigley. She came out, shutting the door behind her.

Steve had his cell phone out. "Got a call from one of our men watching the house in an unmarked car. Looks like a reporter may have found you. If the doorbell rings, don't answer."

"Okay." Claudia began to feel short of breath again.

In less than a minute, the doorbell did ring. Then Claudia's land line rang. Knickerbocker and Jasmine looked up at her, as if wondering what was going on or why she wasn't answering. Steve and Claudia sat down in the living room with one lamp on and the drapes drawn over the front windows.

"From now on I want you to have an unlisted number," Steve admonished her.

"You're right," she replied with a sigh. Though she quietly bristled at being told what to do.

After an hour or so, the doorbell stopped ringing and the answering machine on her phone was full from messages left by various reporters.

"Are you hungry?" Claudia asked. "I have a frozen pizza I can heat up."

Before he could respond, Steve's cell phone buzzed. "O'Rourke." He listened, then turned to Claudia. "Brent Davies showed up at the murder scene. Asked to talk to me. I need to interview him, so I'm going to have a police officer drive him here."

"Lydia Worthington's nephew?" Claudia said with surprise.

"I've been trying to get hold of him."

"Isn't he a possible suspect? You want to bring him here?"

"I don't want to leave you alone in the house," Steve explained. "He'll be patted down for weapons. You'll have to stay in another room though."

"Why?" Claudia found herself increasingly annoyed that he was making arrangements and giving her orders in her own house.

"I'm trying to keep you safe. He doesn't need to know what you look like or that you live here. Though he could figure that out just like reporters have." His tone was kind but stern. "Tomorrow you're going to have that security system installed."

Claudia reluctantly nodded her approval, if that was what he was looking for. He sounded more like he was telling than asking.

Steve relayed his instructions to the police officer on the phone and ended the call.

"You're awfully bossy all of a sudden," she said.

"I'm on duty. Got my detective hat on now. So I need you to follow my instructions."

"Or you'll cuff me and arrest me?"

He gently took her hands in his and turned them palms up, then over, smiling as he studied them. "Your hands are so small and slender, I'd probably have trouble keeping you cuffed."

"That's reassuring," she said, trying for a deadpan manner, but failing. Instead she felt touched and a little giddy as he took her in his arms and nuzzled her cheek.

They were kissing when the doorbell rang. "Briarwood police, escorting Brent Davies," a man's voice announced from the other side of the locked front door.

"Go into the guest room and close the door," Steve told Claudia, releasing her from his embrace.

Claudia's jaw clenched at the bossy manner he'd resumed. She walked into the kitchen as Steve answered the bell.

"He's clean," she could hear the officer tell Steve as she stood next to the stove.

"I'm Detective Steve O'Rourke. Would you come inside? I'd like to interview you."

"About my aunt's murder?" Brent Davies' voice sounded low and serious.

"That's right."

The voices grew easier to hear as Steve apparently admitted Brent into the living room.

"Have a seat while I get out my recorder."

"Am I a suspect?" Brent asked, surprise in his tone. "I went to my Aunt's house hoping to meet you. Saw you on TV."

"Just need to ask you some questions," Steve said.

Claudia decided, since Brent had been declared "clean" and her house was guarded by police inside and outside, that it was safe to go back into the living room. As she did, she pushed the wall switch to turn on the ceiling light, which caused Steve to turn and see her. His face had a mixture of reactions—consternation, worry, and then a new light came into his eyes. Perhaps he was remembering that he'd found her helpful on the two previous murder cases they'd solved together.

She walked up to Brent who had taken a seat in an easy chair, and extended her hand. "I'm Claudia Bailey."

Brent quickly stood, well-dressed in his expensive-looking charcoal suit and silver tie, his auburn hair neat in a conventional cut. He took her hand. "From the Briarwood Cat Clinic? I heard on TV . . . are you the one who has Wrigley?"

"He's in my guest room. Scared, but seems healthy. I wanted to keep him separated from these guys." She looked down to indicate Knickerbocker and Jasmine who had followed her into the living room and were sitting near her feet.

Brent smiled. "Nice looking cats."

"Let's all sit down," Steve said as he placed his digital recorder on the coffee table in front of the couch. Brent sat down again in the nearby easy chair. Claudia settled herself on the other end of the couch from Steve.

Steve turned on the recorder and stated the date, time, place and person he was interviewing.

"I've been trying to reach you," he told Brent. "Have you been out of town?"

"No, but I left work in the morning and was out most of the day with my fiancée. Looking at places to have our wedding reception, tasting cakes and all that kind of thing. I told my secretary to hold my calls and turned off my cell phone. My fiancée wanted my full attention."

"When's the wedding?"

"In eight months."

"Where do you work?"

"I'm a bank manager. Here, I'll give you my card." Brent reached into his inner coat pocket and handed Steve a small business card.

Steve paused as he slipped the card into his suit pocket. "Did you get along well with your aunt, Mrs. Worthington?"

Brent nodded, bowing his head. "We were very close. My parents are gone. She was all that was left of my family."

"How did you learn about Mrs. Worthington's death?"

"On the radio news as I was driving home. I was shocked. Went by her house, but it's all cordoned off. Police wouldn't let me in. I turned on the TV when I got home. Saw your press conference. I decided to go back to the house, hoping to talk to you. Did my aunt really bleed to death from a blow to her head?"

Steve nodded. "Paramedics couldn't revive her."

Brent rubbed his forehead as his eyes grew moist and reddened. "What a horrible way for her to die." He blinked and pulled at the lapels of his suit jacket. "At the press briefing you said Wrigley was missing. And later, that mom and her son said they'd found Wrigley and brought him to Briarwood Clinic. I looked up their website and saw Claudia's name. Glad to know the cat survived the attack."

Claudia studied Brent and sensed that the young man seemed truly bereaved, and that his concern about Wrigley was genuine.

"Mrs. Worthington's lawyer came up to me at the briefing," Steve said. "He told me that she had made an appointment to see him tomorrow, because she wanted to change her will. Did you know that?"

Claudia's head went back. This was a piece of information Steve hadn't mentioned. She drew in a breath. Had Brent wanted to stop his aunt from changing her will?

"Yes, I knew that," Brent replied. "Aunt Lydia always confided in me and asked my advice."

159

"Do you know what modification she wanted to make?" Steve asked.

"She wanted to amend it to leave something for her longtime housekeeper, Maria Kowalski."

Claudia said, "She always told TV reporters she was going to leave her estate to—"

"To Wrigley." Brent chuckled in a nostalgic way. "No, she assured me I would be her main beneficiary. She just told reporters that because she thought it added to Wrigley's celebrity. And she wanted to leave him under my care, after she passed." He sighed. "So . . . can I see Wrigley?"

Claudia looked at Steve. "Should I bring the cat out?"

"Sure." He turned to Brent. "While she's doing that, can you give me the names of the places you and your fiancée visited this afternoon?"

"Be happy to," Brent replied and began naming them.

Claudia walked to the guest room, and Knickerbocker and Jasmine followed her. Wanting to avoid trouble between them and the new feline they perceived as an interloper, Claudia picked them up, one at a time, and carried them to her bedroom, then closed the door on them. She went to the guest room and found Wrigley sitting on the bed in front of his cage. He meowed loudly at her when she walked in, looking up at her anxiously.

"It's okay," she told him, though she reminded herself he was deaf. "Let's go see Brent," she said as she picked him up. He turned in her arms to face

160

her, setting his paws on her shoulders, purring loudly. He'd done this after she'd given him a bath at the clinic, dried him with a blow dryer, and given him some cat treats. Instead of being frightened, he'd seemed comforted to be looked after.

She carried Wrigley, still clinging to her, into the living room. Brent stood when he saw them. He scratched Wrigley behind one ear and the cat turned to him. Brent held out his curled forefinger so the cat could smell him.

"It's me," he said. "How are you doing, buddy?" Brent looked at Claudia. "He can't hear me, but I talk to him anyway."

Claudia chuckled. "I do, too." She was happy to see the cat lick Brent's finger. "He recognizes you. You want to hold him?"

Brent reached to take the cat, but Wrigley ignored him and clung to Claudia.

"He wants you," Brent observed.

"Since he saw his owner murdered by a man who also tried to kidnap him, maybe he's scared of men right now." Claudia glanced at Steve, who looked at her with warmth in his eyes.

"Would you be willing to keep Wrigley?" Brent asked her.

Astonished, Claudia replied, "But your aunt wanted him left in your care. She may have written that into her will."

Brent nodded in a thoughtful way. "I know. But Emily, my fiancée, is allergic to cats. She likes Wrigley, but whenever we stopped by my aunt's,

161

Emily would start sneezing. Aunt Lydia was healthy. We thought she'd go on for years and outlive Wrigley. I don't think we can have him at home with us because of Emily's allergy."

Claudia listened, still flabbergasted. "But doesn't he belong to you legally?"

Brent's brows formed a vertical crease as he seemed to ponder a moment. "How about if I write up a bill of sale and sell him to you for a dollar?"

"What about his Cubs prognostications?" Steve asked.

"That would be up to Claudia," Brent replied. "I can make a statement to the press that she will be handling that from now on." He looked at Claudia. "If you want to, that is."

Claudia eyed Steve. "We can think about that later."

"Right. We have a murder to solve first," Steve said.

"I agree." Brent faced Steve squarely. "So . . . am I still a suspect?"

"I'll verify your whereabouts at the time of the murder," Steve replied. "You're free to go. I'll have an officer drive you back to the Worthington house. I assume you left your car there."

"I did," Brent said. "Thanks. Do you have any clue who murdered my aunt?"

"We're still investigating," Steve told him. "Her home wasn't broken into, so it seems she knew the person. Or else the murderer had a key and knew her home's security code. Do you have any idea who might have killed her?"

"Maria Kowalski had her key and code. She came a few times a week to houseclean. But my aunt trusted her for fifteen years or more. She's a middle-aged, sweet lady."

"It was a male who ran out with the cat," Steve said. "Did your aunt have a gardener?"

"Yes, but I doubt she would have given him access into her house."

"One more question. Did your aunt have any Tarot cards?"

Brent's forehead puckered. "You mean those fortune-telling cards with pictures on them? Not that I know of. She played bridge with her friends. Come to think of it, today would have been her bridge day. Ordinarily she would have been at her friend Mrs. Murphy's this morning. Maybe the game was cancelled and that's why she was home."

"If the intruder knew her habits, he may have expected her to be out," Steve conjectured.

"But she was home," Brent said in a grave tone. "Knowing my aunt, she would have put up a big fight to keep anyone from taking Wrigley."

"Do you know if Maria Kowalski used Tarot cards?" Steve asked.

Claudia stood there holding Wrigley and listened intently over the cat's loud purr, mystified as to why Steve was asking about Tarot cards.

Brent slowly shook his head. "I only met Maria a few times. She seemed pretty down-to-earth. No idea what her interests are. Why? Did you find a deck of Tarot cards at the house?"

"Only one card. It looks old and the words are written in a foreign language. One of my men thought it might be Polish."

"Mrs. Kowalski has an accent," Brent said.

"If anything else comes to mind, let me know." Steve offered his hand.

"I will." Brent shook Steve's hand, then turned to Claudia. "I'll leave Wrigley with you then. You're his new 'mom.'"

"Let me know who his veterinarian has been," Claudia said. "I'll ask for his records."

"Will do." Brent nodded goodbye, gave Wrigley a last scratch behind the ear and walked out the front door.

Steve followed to talk to the police outside, then came back in. After locking the door, he walked up to Claudia. "So now you have three cats."

Claudia shook her head as she smiled. "Hope the other two will accept him."

As she held Wrigley, the white cat stared at her, eye to eye, in a profound way. Like he knew more than he should for a cat. Maybe it was due to the trauma he'd endured.

"You mentioned a pizza?" Steve said.

"Shall I put it in the oven?"

"Might as well. We can't go out and I'd rather not have strangers coming here delivering take-out."

Claudia carried Wrigley back to the guest room. She opened her bedroom door and let Jasmine and Knickerbocker out. Both sat by the closed guest room door like furry sentinels.

Later, Claudia and Steve finished the last pieces of pizza. "I was surprised to hear about the Tarot card," she said, wondering why he hadn't mentioned it to her earlier.

"It was found on the floor near the broken crystal vase."

"Seems odd to find just the one card. Anything else you forgot to tell me?"

He paused and made a half-smile that caused an attractive crease in his cheek. "In the rush to keep you safe, I guess I did forget. Sorry." He stared at her in a fond way. "On this case, you're both a help and a distraction."

She quietly thought through his comment, then decided to let it go. "What will you do next?"

"Interview the housekeeper. Want to come? Your presence might put a middle-aged lady at ease. We found Mrs. Worthington's address book. Shouldn't be hard to locate Maria Kowalski."

"Guess I really am connected with this case," Claudia said, still thinking it unusual to be asked to go along on a police investigation. "It's been nearly six months since we solved the Radek murder, and I acquired Jasmine."

"I like having you along," he said matter-of-factly. "I'm happy that you're part of my life."

Claudia drew in a breath. "I like being with you, too. Dating. It's been good."

His brown eyes connected with hers, growing more intense. "We could . . . you know . . . make it permanent."

She sensed he meant marriage and found herself not wanting to take the hint. "We have a great relationship as it is."

He smiled and looked down. "What's that old Supremes song? Something about not hurrying love." His eyes met Claudia's with indulgent resignation. "I'm happy just being with you."

Claudia tried to hide her discombobulation. *He said the L word. Oh, gosh. Change the subject.* "I think I have some ice cream in the freezer. Want some?"

"Why not?" Steve said in an affable way. "Ice cream is always the great comforter."

Chapter 4: A Whole Other Ball Game

"So why don't you marry him?" Amy asked, pushing her red curly hair back with a show of impatience. "He loves you. How do you feel about him?"

Claudia began to wonder if she should have agreed to meet her old friend for lunch at the Bumblebee Café. Or if she should have confided what Steve said last night. Amy was often a little too direct and sometimes showed an inclination to want to run Claudia's life. She'd known Claudia too long and too well, that was the problem.

"That's just it. I . . . I don't exactly know how I feel." Claudia stirred her spoon in her barely touched mushroom barley soup. "I mean, I like him. A lot. But love is . . . that's a whole other ball game."

Amy's eyes crinkled with amusement. "Okay, that's easy. Now that you're Wrigley's new 'mom,' why don't you ask the cat? He predicts baseball games."

"Oh, ha ha," Claudia wasn't in the mood for jokes.

"You're pushing forty, so you can't take forever to decide. He might not wait."

Claudia set her spoon down and straightened her back. "But I've gotten used to being single. Set in my ways, I suppose. It was a mental adjustment for me to have him stay over last night. He meant to protect me, I get that. But he started giving me orders in my own home. Even if I wanted to marry again, I'm not sure he's good husband material. I've never liked high-handed men."

"Oh, come on. He's a cop who decided to personally assign himself to protect the woman he loves. So he did what he needed to do. And he's patient when you fend off any hint that he's about to propose. He respects you." Amy shook her head in frustration. "How can you pass up this wonderful man?"

"You're too romantic," Claudia chided her friend. "Look, there's a statistic that says married men live longer than single men. But single women live longer than married women. I think that shows who has to absorb the most stress in a marriage. Men like to be in control. I loved my husband. He was very sweet, but even with him, there was some of that male-dominance thing going on."

"Testosterone," Amy said. "It's in their blood. Just talk back."

Claudia ignored her and continued making her point. "It was a bewildering adjustment to find myself widowed and single again. But I've become very happy these last years, paddling my own canoe."

Amy gave her an I-can't-believe-you look. "So your life plan is to live to a ripe old age alone? Be an elderly cat lady?"

With consternation, Claudia realized she didn't exactly know what she was trying to say. She didn't have any life plan. Fortunately a further argument came to mind. "Here's another issue. Steve carries a gun and has to take risks in the line of duty. I don't like the possibility of being widowed again. Once was enough."

Amy looked at her squarely. "None of us knows the future. Steve might live to ninety-five. So could you. Will you want to look back on your life and remember the man you let get away, because you couldn't make a decision?"

Claudia pressed her lips together, getting really annoyed. "Well, I took my time thinking over whether I wanted to marry my first husband. That's just the way I make decisions, slowly and carefully."

Amy's eyes grew big. "Did you hear what you just said?"

"What?"

"You said your *first* husband. Which implies there's going to be a second husband."

Claudia replayed her own words in her mind. "I did say that, didn't I . . . ?"

"So down deep you may already be thinking you'll marry Steve."

Dumbfounded, Claudia could find no coherent reply. Her body hummed with a strange, but energizing nervousness.

#

That evening, after the clinic closed, Steve picked up Claudia and drove to Maria Kowalski's two-story apartment building on the edge of Briarwood.

After Steve rang her doorbell, a thin, sixtyish woman with salt-and-pepper hair opened the door and looked at them with serious brown eyes.

Steve had his badge in hand and showed it to her. "Steve O'Rourke, Briarwood Police. This is Claudia Bailey. She's familiar with this case, and she's caring for Wrigley the cat."

"I'm Maria." She motioned with her hand in a shy but cordial way. "Come in, please."

She invited them to have a seat on her beige couch that had a colorful afghan over the back. Maria settled herself in a padded, oak rocking chair, facing them. A basket of knitting sat on the carpeted floor next to her rocker. The scent of cooked cabbage emanated from the kitchen.

Claudia gazed at the lace curtains on the tall windows at the end of the small living room and the pots of healthy looking violets on a long, narrow table in front of the windows. "You must have a green thumb," she said to Maria. "I tried, but never could keep violets alive. Pretty curtains, too."

"Thank you. My mother grew violets and I learned from her." Maria spoke with a rich accent, but her English was easy to understand. "The curtains are old. My mother brought them with her when my parents and I moved here from Poland long ago. My parents are gone now. So is my husband. Old family keepsakes are a comfort to me."

Claudia looked at Steve, who seemed to be listening with patient interest, though she knew he had important questions for Maria. She noted that he didn't seem to mind waiting for a distinctly female conversation to finish. *Okay, maybe he's not such a high-handed male after all.*

Steve smiled slightly and looked at Maria. "As I told you on the phone, Briarwood Police are investigating Mrs. Worthington's death. I need to ask you some questions."

Maria nodded. "I understand. She was my favorite client. Hard to believe she's gone."

Steve took out his digital recorder and turned it on. After stating the pertinent info, he set it on the polished wood side table next to the couch, beneath a lit lamp with a fringed shade.

"How long have you worked for Mrs. Worthington?"

"Sixteen years."

"You had a key to her house? Did you know her home's security code?"

"Yes, she trusted me with her key and gave me the code. She served on several charity boards, so she was often out at meetings, and I needed to get in when she wasn't home. She only turned on the security system when she went out of town." Maria's face softened with nostalgia. "She wanted a spotless home and it's quite a big house. She liked to host catered dinner parties. So I would come to clean twice, sometimes three times a week, depending on her plans."

"You got along well?" Steve asked.

"Always, from the first time I met her. One of her woman friends recommended me."

"How about her cat?"

Maria's mouth curved into a small smile. "Wrigley and I were pals. He'd get lonely when she wasn't home, so he followed me around the house as I cleaned. I'd pet him when I stopped to take a break." She looked at Claudia. "I'm glad he's being taken care of."

"Do you have other clients you clean for?" Steve asked.

"I used to, but the last few years I've only worked for Mrs. W." Maria chuckled. "I called her that, and she didn't mind. She gave me a generous raise, and I was able to make ends meet with her as my only client."

As she sat, quietly listening, Claudia thought this a bit odd. "Even with the nice raise, wouldn't it still be better to have had at least one other client? You had a few days available when you weren't at Mrs. Worthington's. And now you have no clients?"

Maria slowly nodded and looked at her hands, gnarled from arthritis, in her lap. "I'm not as spry as I used to be. My back gives me trouble sometimes. So I see a chiropractor one day a week. And I often have other doctor's appointments, too. But you're right, I need to find some new people to clean for."

Claudia felt empathy for the woman's situation. "Have you thought of maybe having a young person help you? A high school student looking to earn a little money, for example."

Maria stared at Claudia with a stunned expression and straightened up in her rocking chair. "No. I prefer to work alone."

Claudia and Steve shared a glance. She sensed he was on the same wavelength noticing Maria's change in demeanor.

Steve resumed questioning the lady. "Where were you on the morning Mrs. Worthington was killed?"

"At my chiropractor, all morning." Maria seemed to relax and grew talkative again. "Had to wait. His office is always crowded. He put me on an ice pack for a long while, and then did adjustments on my spine. And traction. I can give you his number, so you can verify it."

"Yes, I'd like the number." Reaching into his pocket, Steve pulled out a card encased in a clear plastic evidence bag. He held it up. "Have you ever seen this before?"

Maria gaped open-mouthed at the card, her face growing pale. "Yes." She swallowed. "It's a Tarot card. From a deck that was my grandmother's in Poland. How . . . where did you get it?"

"On the floor of Mrs. Worthington's living room. Between her dead body and a broken crystal vase," Steve said, matter-of-factly.

"Oh, no . . . no." Maria weakly lifted her trembling hand to her face.

"Are you all right?" Claudia worried that the lady might faint.

Maria folded her arms over her chest, hugging herself as she seemed to try to pull herself together. "I'm all right."

"Any idea how the card got there?" Steve asked. "Do you usually carry the deck of Tarot cards with you?"

"No. Never. They're a keepsake from my grandmother. The deck is in a drawer in my bedroom." She pointed to a doorway to her left. "I don't know why that card would be at Mrs. W's."

"Would you be willing to show us the deck of cards?" Steve asked.

With deliberation, Maria stiffly pushed herself up from her rocking chair, walked into the other room, and came back with a set of cards held together with an old rubber band. She handed them to Steve.

Steve took off the rubber band, and he and Claudia quickly looked through the cards. Claudia marveled at how timeworn they appeared to be, graying around their soft edges, some with stains. But the colors of the arcane drawings were still vivid.

"Are the words beneath the pictures written in Polish?" Claudia asked.

Maria nodded.

Steve had left the card found at Mrs. Worthington's house lying on his knee. Claudia picked it up and tried to figure out the printed drawing. The picture showed a yellow hoop with a blindfolded woman in a medieval dress in the middle, her arms stretched to hold onto the hoop. She seemed to be standing on the back of an ancient white-haired man who was on all fours. On her left and right were two people clinging to the hoop, one of them upside down. Above her head stood another human figure. At the bottom were the words *Kolo Fortuny*.

"Can you translate?" Claudia asked Maria, turning the card toward her. "What's the meaning of this particular one?"

"It's the Wheel of Fortune." A grimace creased Maria's lined face. "It's often interpreted to mean good luck. A change in life." Her composure faltered. "But it can mean bad luck, too."

"Any reason why this card would have gotten separated from the deck?" Steve asked.

Maria lowered her gaze. "No idea," she replied. She looked up at Steve, her eyes sharp. "Are we done? You have more to ask?"

Steve studied her and seemed to ponder a moment. "Not at this time, but I may want to speak to you again." He took the Wheel of Fortune card from Claudia. "I'll hold onto this," he told Maria. "It's evidence. We had it tested for fingerprints."

Maria's eyes widened with alarm. "You did? But . . . mine are on it."

175

"I'll send someone to take yours for comparison. If your chiropractor verifies that you were at his office at the time of the murder, then you'll be cleared. But the card has more than one person's prints on it."

"I'm sure. It's been in my family for a century." Maria sounded surprisingly defensive. "My grandmother's prints must be on it. She loved to do Tarot readings. She died forty years ago."

"Fingerprint experts know what they're doing," Steve quietly told her. He slipped the card into his jacket pocket and handed the Tarot deck to Maria. Rising from the couch, he told her, "Appreciate your help. If you think of anything that might be useful in solving this case, give me a call." He handed her his Briarwood Police card.

Maria stood and dutifully accepted his card. She walked with them to the door and said goodbye.

As they drove away in Steve's unmarked car, Claudia asked, "What do you think about Maria?"

"I think she knows more than she's saying."

"Me, too. Like how the Tarot card made its way to Mrs. Worthington's. And she seemed defensive about the idea of working with someone else. I wonder why."

"Right." He glanced at her. "I'm glad you came along. You put her at ease asking about her violets."

"Until you showed her the Wheel of Fortune card. She turned pale. I thought she might pass out."

Steve slowly nodded. "I think that's the key. Have you ever had a Tarot reading?"

"No. I'm not into that kind of thing."

"Me, either. But I'm kind of curious about it now."

"Really?"

"Maybe a Tarot expert could tell me if my life will change for the better."

Claudia felt hesitant, but found herself asking, "In what way?"

"Oh, say, if a legal license and a church ceremony that decrees a change from singular to plural are in my future."

Here he goes again! Claudia rolled her eyes, stymied as to how to respond.

"Just saying. Wondering if it's in the cards." Steve's tone was airy. "So, where should we stop for dinner? In the mood for Italian? Chinese? A burger?"

Claudia wasn't particularly hungry, but relieved he'd changed the subject. She almost replied *Chinese*, but remembered fortune cookies would be served. Steve could probably interpret any cryptic fortune he might get as a cue for marriage.

She grew still as all at once she recalled a curious thing. A year ago or more, she'd had lunch at a Chinese restaurant. When she'd opened her cookie, her fortune read: *You are doomed to be happy in wedlock.*

"Any suggestion?" Steve prompted.

"Italian," Claudia quickly answered.

Chapter 5: The Funeral

On the following Saturday, the funeral for Lydia Worthington was held at the largest church in Briarwood. Claudia drove there from the cat clinic and met Steve in the parking lot. She hadn't worn scrubs that day and instead had put on a long black skirt and a blouse with a floral print against a black background. She'd twisted her long hair into a French braid.

"You look very nice!" Steve said as she walked up to where he was waiting near the entrance to the church lot.

"Thank you. So do you. New suit?"

"Store had a sale, so I took advantage." He straightened his striped tie worn with a crisply tailored grey pinstripe suit. "Shall we go in and find seats? The pews will fill up."

As they began walking up the steps toward the church's large double doors, Claudia noticed there was a Briarwood police presence. One uniformed man stood near the parking lot entrance, another on the sidewalk in front of the building, one on the church steps, and a police car had pulled up at the corner of the cross streets where the historic church stood.

"Are you expecting trouble?" Claudia asked, after she saw Steve nod to the young police officer standing guard on the church steps.

"Just a precaution. Mrs. Worthington was murdered—and well-known—so a crowd is expected. People may come out of curiosity."

As they entered the church, a uniformed female officer stood in the church entry hall. They went into the sanctuary and walked down the center aisle. Claudia noticed a group of men and women, all wearing blue Cubs T-shirts with the team's circular logo, sitting in the very back two rows on the right side. Their casual attire made a contrast with all the well-dressed people entering or already seated.

Smiling, Claudia whispered to Steve, "I wonder if they're hoping to see Wrigley here."

Steve laughed. "How's he doing, by the way?"

"Okay. I called his vet and found out his dry food is duck and green pea. He's been eating, but he's quiet. Still traumatized. He likes to be near me. I haven't let the other cats in to see him yet. But they hang around the guest room door a lot."

"He'll be your most famous house guest." Steve motioned toward a few empty seats in a row about one third down from the back of the church. People already seated moved over so Steve and Claudia could sit at the end of the upholstered wooden pew. An organ was playing and a closed white casket had been placed at the front, near the altar. Next to the casket was an enlarged color photo of Lydia Worthington holding Wrigley on her lap. Several large floral arrangements added beauty and the fragrance of roses.

Claudia perused the program she'd been handed by an usher. As she read, she began to feel cold and knew that soon she'd be shivering. "They have the air conditioning turned up so high," she quietly said to Steve. "I keep an old sweater in my car. Be back in a minute."

Steve turned as she got up, concern in his eyes. "I can go with you."

"I'll be fine." She grinned. "The place is crawling with cops."

Claudia hurried down the aisle in her high heels, walked outside and headed to the parking lot at the side of the building. She found her Prius, got her white sweater out of the back seat, and locked her car. As she turned to go back, a plump, brown-haired, middle-aged woman, wearing black pants and a Cubs T-shirt, approached her with hesitance.

"Hi," the woman said, her tone and demeanor apologetic. "I noticed you walk in with that detective I saw on TV. O'Reilly, is that his name?"

"O'Rourke." Claudia wasn't fearful of the woman, but wondered what she wanted.

"Right, Detective O'Rourke. Um, look, I can't get involved. Hope no one sees me talking to you." She turned to glance behind her, then held out a tightly folded copy of the program for the funeral. "I wrote a note for the detective, hoping to get it to him. Saw you leave. Would you please give this to him? Don't point me out. I don't want trouble. Okay?"

"Is the note about Mrs. Worthington's murder?" Claudia asked.

The woman held her forefinger to her lips. "Shh." She nodded *yes*. "Have to get back to my group. We sit together in the bleachers at Wrigley Field. Said I was going to the ladies' room. So, thanks. Goodbye!" She hurried off.

"Wait. What's your name?" Claudia called.

The woman ignored the question and increased her pace. Soon she'd gone around the corner of the building and was out of sight.

Claudia opened up the folded program that felt damp from sweat. Inside, scribbled in pencil, she read: *Art Clingenpeel. Red hair, sunglasses. Cubs shirt & cap. Back row. Lost $ on Wrigley prediction. Says wants to kill cat. Suspect?*

Claudia refolded the program and hid it in the pocket of her skirt, then walked back into the church carrying her sweater. People were still entering as the large sanctuary, much bigger and more ornate than Claudia's church could boast, grew increasingly crowded. As she passed the last two pews where the Cubs fans were seated, she faced forward and gave them a sidelong glance. She caught sight of a man with long red hair and sunglasses at the end of the back row by the side aisle. Sitting in the middle of the pew in front of him, she saw the woman who had snuck out to pass her the note.

Claudia took her seat beside Steve, who helped her wrap her sweater around her shoulders. "A woman in the Cubs group gave me this," she whispered, glad the organ music was still playing. She pulled the program out of her pocket and opened it so he could see the penciled note.

Steve took it and read it.

"I saw a guy of that description in the back row, side aisle." Claudia looked at Steve. "What do we do?"

Steve seemed to be thinking as he refolded the note and stuck it in his jacket pocket. "He might get lost in the crowd when the service ends. I better approach him now. You stay here."

He rose and headed down the middle aisle, dodging people entering, and disappeared into the entry hall. Claudia turned her gaze toward the back door leading to the side aisle and in a moment Steve appeared. He looked over the Cubs fans and leaned down to say something to the red-haired man wearing sunglasses. Steve showed his badge and Art Clingenpeel's muscular shoulders stiffened. With a churlish countenance, he got up and walked ahead of Steve out the door.

Claudia couldn't just sit in her pew and wait. She rose and headed toward the back to try to quietly observe what happened. When she reached the entry hall, she saw Steve escorting the tall man to the outside steps. And then, all at once, Clingenpeel took off running.

"Stop! Police!" Steve yelled in an authoritative voice as he began chasing him.

The uniformed policeman on the steps immediately followed. Steve caught up and in a swift move brought Clingenpeel face down on the grass while people entering the church stared. Impressed at Steve's strength and agility, Claudia walked closer. She stood nearby as the uniformed cop handcuffed Clingenpeel while Steve kept him pinned down.

The fugitive was still struggling, kicking his feet. "Why are you cuffing me?"

"Need to ask you some questions," Steve said. "About the murder of Mrs. Worthington."

"Huh? I'm no murderer!"

"I hear you threatened to kill Wrigley the cat."

"I didn't do nothin' to that fricken cat!"

"Why did you run?" Steve asked.

The man gritted his teeth and didn't reply.

"You're coming to the station with us," Steve told him. He and the officer lifted him to his feet and escorted him to the waiting police car, just as other squad cars were pulling up in front of the church.

Claudia stayed where she was, catching her breath. She realized she hadn't been breathing, because she'd gotten scared watching Steve physically apprehend the man. After Clingenpeel had gotten into the car, Steve looked back and saw her. He hurried over to say, "Have to go. Stay here and let me know if you see or hear anything else."

"Are you all right?" She looked him over and pointed a shaking finger at his sleeve. "You got grass stains on your new suit."

He grinned. "I'll send it to the cleaners. You sound like a wife."

She blinked. "Well, I got worried when I saw you tackle that big guy."

"About me or my suit?"

"About you, silly." She made an effort to smile. "But I see you know how to take care of yourself."

He looked at her, new lights playing in his eyes. "Claudia, I'd really love to continue this conversation, but I have to interview this guy." Steve squeezed her hand. "Later," he said and headed toward his car.

Claudia sat through the service, having trouble concentrating at first. She had to admit to herself that she cared more deeply about Steve than she realized. *Am I in love? What else would describe what I feel?* But the thought unsettled her, and she decided to think it through later.

She was finally able to focus when Brent walked up to the front to speak. He gave a touching eulogy about his aunt and her devotion to charitable causes, to the Cubs, and her beloved Wrigley.

Claudia began to worry about the fact that she'd become Wrigley's caretaker—a more comfortable worry than examining her feelings for Steve. The cat was surely missing his favorite person, had probably seen Mrs. Worthington murdered. Would he recover? And what about the

184

Cubs fans? Would they want him to continue predicting baseball games?

After the service, as she was leaving, she saw the woman who had given her the scribbled note. But when she noticed Claudia looking at her, she quickly turned and brushed past people to dash out. Claudia figured she didn't want to be identified as the snitch who told on a fellow Cubs fan. With his height and red hair, Clingenpeel matched the general description of the man seen trying to carry off Wrigley, so Claudia could understand why the woman wanted to remain anonymous.

As she walked toward the parking lot, Brent caught up with her.

"Thanks for coming to the service," he said. "How's Wrigley?"

"Your tribute to your aunt was lovely," she told him. "Wrigley's doing okay. He had a limp, but that's gone now. He's still not feeling at home. I'm going to gradually introduce him to my other two cats." A thought came to her. "Brent, would you mind if I got Wrigley's toys and things from Mrs. Worthington's house? If he had familiar objects around him, it would help."

"Absolutely," Brent replied. "Excellent idea. But the house is still a crime scene. Maybe Detective O'Rourke can get you in. My aunt kept a lot of Wrigley's things in her bedroom upstairs. He'd stay in her room at night."

"Okay, thanks." Claudia felt relieved that she could do something to comfort Wrigley.

"Thank *you*," he said. "I'm glad Wrigley will be looked after by such a caring person."

They parted with a hand-shake. Claudia was deep in thought as she entered the parking lot, along with a crowd of other people going to their cars. Someone tapped her on the shoulder. She turned to find Maria Kowalski, dressed in black, looking at her with tired, dark-circled eyes.

"Maria. I didn't see you in the church."

"I sat in the balcony. Is Detective O'Rourke here?"

"He had to leave."

Maria bowed her head, her shoulders scrunched in a guilty manner. "There's something I should have told him. My young cousin, Stanislaus, has been helping me houseclean over the summer. I didn't like it known that my bad back is making it hard to do my job. He was helping me in return for letting him stay at my apartment."

"So he was familiar with Mrs. Worthington's house. Did he have a key? What about the security code?"

"We used my key. I suppose he might have seen the code numbers as I punched them in. But Mrs. W only turned on the security system when she was out of town. She'd been home the last few weeks. Stanislaus is a good boy," she insisted. "Not the smartest young man, but wouldn't hurt anyone."

"Would he know about the missing Tarot card?"

The lines in Maria's face seemed to grow deeper. "He had it. I should have told you. He thought it meant good luck. But I'm sure he dropped it as he vacuumed or something. I know how it looks, but I can't believe he'd murder anyone. He's never had a bad temper or been violent. Why would he want to kill Mrs. W?"

Claudia took out her cell phone. "You'll need to tell Detective O'Rourke all this."

Chapter 6: All In a Day's Work

As Claudia, Maria and Steve sat in a small, plain, conference room at the Briarwood Police Station, Steve listened as Maria told him everything she'd confessed to Claudia.

"Stanislaus sleeps on my couch. Or sometimes he stays at a friend's house. He's a janitor at Briarwood Grade School, but school's closed for the summer, so he's temporarily out of work. He can't afford an apartment. I offered to have him help me houseclean in exchange for staying with me and cooking some meals for him. I give him a little money, too. I'm sure he must have accidentally dropped the Tarot card the last time we housecleaned for Mrs. W. That was the day before she was murdered."

"If you were cleaning, wouldn't you have noticed the card littering the living room floor?" Steve asked.

Maria lifted her shoulders. "I don't know why we didn't. I trusted Stanislaus to vacuum the Persian rug in that room and sweep the hardwood floor while I was cleaning the kitchen. I didn't check his work as I should have."

"Why did he carry the Wheel of Fortune card with him?" Claudia asked. "I thought the whole Tarot deck is usually used."

"I showed him the deck because it belonged to his great-grandmother. I told him that each morning she used to draw one card out of the deck as the card for the day. She believed it gave an insight into what the day might have in store. Like reading your horoscope in the newspaper. So Stanislaus shuffled the cards and that was the one he drew. When I told him the Wheel of Fortune could mean good luck, he got all excited. He's always feeling down on his luck, you see. He wants a place of his own, but can't even afford a cell phone. He asked if he could keep the card. I guess he thought of it as a lucky charm. I let him take it. It seemed to make him so happy."

"Where is he now?" Steve asked.

"I don't know. At his friend's maybe," Maria worriedly replied. "I tried calling there, but no answer."

"Do you still have the key to Mrs. Worthington's house?"

Maria opened her black handbag and drew out her key chain. "Here it is," she said, holding up one of the keys.

"Would you describe Stanislaus?" Steve asked. "Have a photo of him?"

"I have a photo." She began searching her purse. "He's fairly tall. Long reddish brown hair. Green eyes."

"Clean-shaven?" Steve asked.

"Yes. Used to have a beard, but he started shaving it. Said it was too hot in the summer." Maria found the snapshot and handed it to Steve.

After looking at it, Steve gave it to Claudia. The photo showed a young man with a narrow face and docile eyes, appearing shy as he posed for the picture standing next to a small Christmas tree. He wore a plaid shirt and jeans.

"Any reason he may have disliked Mrs. Worthington?" Steve asked.

"Absolutely not." Maria grew emphatic. "He never met her. As I said, I wanted to keep it quiet that I was having trouble doing the housework. Stanislaus came with me only when I knew she wouldn't be home."

"Did he like Wrigley?" Claudia asked.

"Wrigley seemed wary of him," Maria admitted. "One time Stanislaus looked at Wrigley and joked that Mrs. W would put up a big reward if Wrigley disappeared. Wrigley stared back at Stanislaus and spit. Stan backed away. It seemed funny at the time, this deaf white cat on the floor hissing and intimidating a grown man."

"I appreciate what you've told us," Steve said. "I'd like to keep this photo for now. Also, if you can find a hair of his on his clothes, or an unwashed glass he drank from, that would help."

"Why?"

"DNA. We could compare it to the blood samples we took off the cat. The blood on Wrigley's paws matches Mrs. Worthington's. But we haven't found a match for the blood around the cat's mouth. If Stanislaus's DNA is different, it would clear his name."

Maria's expression brightened. "All right. I'll bring you his hairbrush."

"And if you hear from Stanislaus, you'll let me know?"

"Of course," Maria said sincerely. "I'm sure he's innocent."

After Maria left, Claudia asked about Art Clingenpeel. "Is he still here?"

"He's in a holding cell downstairs, waiting to be transferred to Cook County Jail," Steve told her. "Chicago police have warrants out for his arrest. He ignored a restraining order and forced his way into his ex-wife's apartment to steal money. And he got into a dispute at a fast food place and threw hot coffee in a guy's face. Security cameras recorded it."

Claudia felt shaken by this news. "He sounds dangerous. Are you sure you're all right after tackling him? I saw the fight he put up."

"All in a day's work." Steve raised his eyebrows. "But I like that you're worrying about me. You must care about me at least as much as you do your cats."

Claudia grew self-conscious, smiling slightly because she felt guilty not wanting to talk about her feelings, and decided to change the subject. "So have you learned where Clingenpeel was at the time of the murder?"

"He wouldn't tell us anything." Steve's demeanor became businesslike again. "Chicago police may be of help."

"Good. By the way, I've been wondering if there's any way you or I could go to Mrs. Worthington's house. I talked to Brent at the funeral and asked if I could get Wrigley's things."

"Cats have things?"

"Sure. Food bowls, toys, even cat furniture."

Steve laughed. "Cat furniture. That's a new one on me. So Brent was okay with that?"

"He seemed happy that I'm trying to make Wrigley feel secure. Can you go and get them? Or can we go together?"

"You'd better come with me. I might not recognize all of Wrigley's prized belongings."

She quirked her mouth and gave him a look. "Come on. You said you once had a dog. Didn't he have a few toys? A mat to sleep on? A leash?"

Steve slipped his arm around her waist. "You're right, he did. I'd forgotten. Want to go over there now? I had the day off to attend the funeral. Got sidetracked, but I'm free now. You have the rest of the day, too, don't you?"

"Let's go," she happily replied.

Chapter 7: A Pair of Men's Shoes

As she walked into Mrs. Worthington's big living room, Claudia immediately noticed that an elegant green velvet sofa had been pushed out of place by a large, gold and glass coffee table that appeared to have been shoved into it. A crystal vase, which perhaps had been on the table, lay on the floor broken. Dried blood that had soaked into the plush Persian rug beneath the table and sofa, still showed paw prints. A pool of blood, dry now, with paw prints extended a few feet onto the polished hardwood floor. A lamp beside the sofa had been overturned.

Claudia stared at it all, tears welling in her eyes. "This is awful."

Steve gave her a comforting hug. "Don't look at it. Go upstairs and search for Wrigley's things. I'll stay down here and re-examine the scene."

Claudia wiped her eyes and climbed the curved staircase. At the end of the landing, she found what appeared to be Mrs. Worthington's spacious bedroom. She stepped in and discovered an inviting window seat in the recess of a bow window that jutted out above her rose garden. The bed had a silk coverlet and lots of big pillows in aqua and coral prints. She walked across the champagne colored carpet to the coral velvet window seat, on which she found several cat toys—a stuffed cloth mouse, a ping pong ball, a feathered toy bird, and some multi-colored bows that looked like they came off of presents. Nearby she found a cushioned, fleece-lined basket that Wrigley must have napped in. White fur still clung to it. She also found a plastic tubular ring, about a foot in diameter, with holes where a cat could bat at the ball that rolled through it.

Claudia picked up the toys, put them in the cat bed, and took them out to the landing. She looked down into the living room, where Steve seemed preoccupied examining the corner of the coffee table.

"Found Wrigley's things," she told Steve.

He glanced up. "Good. Need help carrying anything?"

"No, thanks." She paused a moment and gazed over the living room below, admiring the artistically painted Chinese screen decorating a corner of the room. She wondered if Mrs. Worthington had bought it on a trip to Asia. Then, to Claudia's shock, she noticed a pair of men's shoes, soles upward, just behind the screen. They could only be viewed from her position on the upstairs landing.

One of the shoes moved, confirming that someone was hiding behind the screen on their hands and knees.

Her heart began to pound with apprehension. "Steve? Maybe I do need help after all."

"Okay." He walked around the couch and climbed the steps. When he reached her, she held

194

her forefinger to her mouth to indicate silence, then pointed to the shoes behind the screen.

He looked in the direction she showed him, eyes narrowing, and took out his cell phone.

Claudia began breathing deeply, gripping the railing along the edge of the landing. He slipped his arm around her and gently pulled her away from the railing.

"Better double-check to make sure you haven't missed any cat toys," he said in an easy tone that was loud enough to be heard downstairs. He led her into the bedroom and whispered, "Stay here." Using his phone, he called for backup, then walked out onto the landing and headed down the staircase.

Claudia remained in the bedroom for about ten seconds. She set down the basket and crept far enough out on the landing to see Steve at the bottom of the steps, his gun drawn.

Steve quietly walked to the edge of the screen where the shoes were and shoved the screen aside, folding it at its hinges. There, a thin man on all fours with red-brown hair looked up in wide-eyed horror at the detective staring down at him, gun in hand.

"I'm Detective O'Rourke, Briarwood Police. Stanislaus?"

"Y-yes."

"Lie flat on the floor. Hands behind your head."

Stanislaus did as he was told. Claudia could see that his left hand was swollen and red.

"Looking for the Tarot card you dropped?" Steve asked him.

"W-what Tarot card?" Stanislaus seemed to try feigning an innocent tone.

"Thought if you found the evidence you left here, you'd escape being charged with the murder of Mrs. Worthington? That bite on your hand would give you away. I'm guessing your DNA will match the blood found on Wrigley's mouth."

Stanislaus's whole body began to tremble. "I didn't mean to hurt her or the cat."

Meanwhile, Claudia heard sirens outside, then a car door slamming. In a few moments, a uniformed blond policeman entered the house as another car could be heard coming to a stop.

Claudia cautiously stepped forward to get a better view.

Steve motioned to the young officer, who pulled out his handcuffs.

To the man on the floor, Steve said in a stern voice, "You're under arrest for murder."

Stanislaus looked to the door, as if wondering if he could somehow make a run for it, but two more cops entered. Steve slipped his gun into the shoulder holster beneath his jacket and began to read Stanislaus his Miranda rights. "You have the right to remain silent—"

The young man's face crumpled. "I didn't mean to kill her," he insisted. "You've got to believe me! She wasn't supposed to be home. I only wanted to take the cat and return it when she offered a reward."

Steve continued reciting. "If you cannot afford a lawyer, one will be appointed to represent you—"

"But she was home," Stanislaus went on in a pleading tone, as if looking for mercy. "She started hitting me with a vase. I pushed her and she fell against the table. I thought she'd come to. I grabbed Wrigley and ran."

Steve had finished the Miranda rights. "Where have you been hiding?" Steve asked. "Maria's been worried."

"In the janitor's closet at the school."

Steve eyed the other officers. They took hold of Stanislaus, lifted him to his feet and walked him out the door. Steve told them he'd be at the police station shortly.

Claudia grabbed the basket of toys she'd left in the bedroom and hurried down the steps. She set it on the couch and threw her arms around Steve. "I'm glad you're okay."

"You did an admirable job tipping me off he was here," Steve said, hugging her.

"How did he get in?" she asked.

"Maybe when he cleaned the house with Maria, he left a window unlocked somewhere. The security system hadn't been set. We'll find out." He took her by the shoulders and gave her a little shake. "Have to go book him. Two culprits in one day. And you helped me get both of them."

"It all seemed accidental on my part," she said. "You're the one doing the dangerous stuff."

"I haven't had to draw my gun in a long time," he said, patting the shoulder holster under his jacket. "Most cops never have to use their weapon." His eyes delved into hers. "Being a detective's spouse might seem scary to you right now. I understand that. But Briarwood has a low crime rate. I could reach retirement never having pulled out my gun again."

She nodded and looked toward the door. *He's sure bringing up marriage a lot.* "It's not exactly the time to discuss that. You have to book Stanislaus."

He smiled, bringing out the attractive creases in his cheeks. "Never seems to be quite the right time." He kissed her. Then he took her by the shoulders and held her away from him. "I'll come by your house later. Would you like to make a reservation for dinner tonight at The Old Mill? To celebrate that we solved the case?"

She blinked, her head still whirling slightly from his surprise kiss. "All right. Six-thirty?"

Chapter 8: Wrigley's Psychic Advice

Steve rang her door bell at about five o'clock that afternoon. It was too early to leave for the restaurant. Claudia invited him in and offered him some iced tea.

As he stepped into her living room, she noticed he'd changed to a different suit, this one blue pinstripe with the yellow and navy plaid tie she'd given him on his birthday a few months ago.

"Hope the cleaners can get rid of the grass stains on your other suit. You look great. Nice tie," she quipped.

"I thought so," he agreed and gave her a kiss. He turned toward the couch. "What's this? Jasmine and Knickerbocker are in the same room with Wrigley?"

The Himalayan and the Maine Coon were staring at them from their napping spots on either side of the back of the sofa. Wrigley had curled up on the seat cushion, his blue eyes alert and wary.

"I've been letting them see each other little by little," Claudia explained with a pleased smile. "There's been some hissing and swatting. But today everything's copacetic. I think they sense that Wrigley is deaf. Yesterday morning I dropped the pot I use to cook oatmeal. They scooted a few feet at the clatter, but Wrigley took no notice. They sat and stared at him. After that they've been more accepting, like letting him share the sofa. They may even feel protective of Wrigley."

"Cats can feel protective?" Steve said with surprise. "I know dogs do."

"Cats have feelings, too. They just hide them more."

Steve nodded thoughtfully. "Maybe that's why you have such an affinity with felines."

Claudia didn't know whether to smile or frown. His perceptive comment made her self-conscious. "Want to come into the kitchen? Iced tea is in the fridge."

"Sounds good." He followed her and sat down at the square kitchen table on which she'd spread Saturday's Chicago Tribune. All three cats followed, too, one by one, their paws silent on the taupe-colored tile floor.

"Have a look at the paper, if you like," she said as she filled two glasses with ice at the quartz-topped counter next to the fridge. "I was checking the end-of-summer sales."

Steve appeared amused as he glanced over the pages opened out to department store ads. "If you don't mind, I'll have a look at the sports section."

Just like a man. "Sure, go ahead." She took a pitcher of tea out of the fridge and poured it over the ice in the glasses.

She set his drink on the table and sat down with hers opposite him.

"Hmm." There was an element of worry in his tone as he perused the paper.

"What? Your favorite team is losing?"

"No," he replied. "Just the opposite. The Cubs will be in the playoffs." He looked up from the sports page on which there was a photo of the Cubs' best pitcher in his uniform. "Fans may be looking for Wrigley to prognosticate."

Claudia raised her fingertips to her mouth. "Oh, no, you're right." She turned to search the floor and found Wrigley sitting near her chair. She reached down to pick him up. Instead of staying on her lap, the cat climbed up onto the table, walking over the sports page.

"What do you think, Wrigley?" Steve asked with jaunty humor. "Should we put you in front of the cameras so you can make predictions on the playoffs?"

Wrigley meowed loudly, looking at Steve and then Claudia. Spreading his paws, he began clawing the photo of the Cubs pitcher, shredding the image and the news article. When he was finished, he walked off the newspaper and sat in a regal pose on a corner of the table, tail wrapped around his paws.

Amazement lit Steve's eyes. "You think he meant that as an answer?"

Claudia looked from Steve to Wrigley, feeling an eerie sort of astonishment. "Hard to take it any other way." She pushed a stray hair off her face. "Well, I can't say I mind his answer."

"Me, either," Steve agreed. "I think all of us would be happier and safer keeping Wrigley out of the spotlight." Steve reached out to scratch the side of the cat's neck, which made Wrigley close his eyes and purr.

Steve straightened his posture, his eyes brightening even more. "Say, why don't we ask Wrigley to prognosticate one last time? Just for us."

Claudia wrinkled her brow. "About the Cubs?"

"No. About us." He looked around the kitchen. She saw his gaze hone in on the bag of duck and green pea cat food sitting on the counter between the refrigerator and the stove.

"About us?" Claudia repeated, perplexed.

"Where do you keep clean cat food bowls?" He rose to grab the bag of food, then began opening her cupboard doors.

"Bottom shelf, door on the left," she said with some impatience. *Here he goes taking over my kitchen, and he won't even say for what.*

In no time, he had shoved away the newspaper, set two small white bowls in the middle of the table, and poured cat food into each one. Wrigley watched with keen interest. Steve took a pen from his pocket, tore off two small pieces of newspaper, and wrote *Yes* on one and *No* on the other. He arranged them in front of the bowls.

"What on earth are you doing?" she asked.

"Asking Wrigley for his psychic advice." He lifted the cat to its feet and set him in front of the

202

two bowls. He got in front of the blue-eyed feline and said, "Wrigley, should Claudia marry Steve?"

"What?!" Claudia exclaimed.

"Shh. See which bowl he chooses," Steve told her in a hushed voice.

"This is ridiculous," Claudia objected, her dander rising.

"Let's just see what he does."

Wrigley crouched in front of the white dishes, sniffing the *Yes* bowl and then the *No* bowl. He began eating out of the *No* bowl.

"Oh." Steve stared at the cat, his shoulders slumping.

Claudia found herself neither happy nor unhappy, just bewildered. If she really didn't want to marry again, shouldn't she feel relieved? "This is just stupid, Steve. We don't need a cat predicting our future."

"But Wrigley is right eighty-two percent of the time," Steve said.

"Well, that means he's wrong eighteen percent of the time. Isn't that why Clingenpeel wanted to wring Wrigley's neck, because he'd bet on a prediction that the cat got wrong?"

"Still," Steve said in a surprisingly sensible tone, "he's got a very good track record. You know, I think Wrigley may be right. Marriage may not be our best option."

Claudia drew her brows together. *He's sure singing a different tune all of a sudden!* She glanced at the table. "Look, Wrigley's eating out of the *Yes* bowl now."

"That doesn't count," Steve said. "You have to go by his first choice."

Claudia rolled her eyes. "Maybe he's confused. He never made predictions on a kitchen table in front of only two people. And two cats."

Jasmine and Knickerbocker had been keenly observing from the floor. As if of one mind, they jumped onto the table and began eating out of the bowls as Wrigley, apparently full, leapt off the table.

"Well, everybody's predicting now." Annoyed, Claudia looked at her watch. "Shouldn't we be leaving for the restaurant?"

Steve's eyes grew keen with renewed energy. "You bet. Let's go." He looked at her in a meaningful way—a meaning only he understood.

What on earth is going on with him? Claudia grabbed her handbag and followed him out. *What happened to the sensible, down-to-earth detective I thought I knew?*

Chapter 9: Dinner at The Old Mill

The Old Mill was bustling, as usual, on a Saturday evening. To Claudia's surprise, they were shown to a table by the window that looked onto the garden and the stream on which the century-old, wooden mill wheel turned. The historic mill had been refurbished and turned into a restaurant in the 1970's, and had prospered in its new form ever since.

Claudia looked out at the grassy stream where Mallard ducks floated by. She felt calmed from her earlier displeasure at Steve asking Wrigley for a prediction on whether they should marry, and his odd reaction when Wrigley chose *no*. Maybe Steve meant the whole thing in fun. Except somehow she didn't think it was funny. *That's over. Time to enjoy dinner.*

"I never expected to get such a prize table," she said. "I didn't ask for anything special when I made the reservation."

Steve didn't seem surprised. "Guess we lucked out." He opened his menu. "How about some champagne?"

"Really?" Claudia lifted her shoulders. "Okay. We didn't celebrate the other cases we solved this much."

"Time to start a new tradition."

"You mean I'll keep getting involved in murder cases?" Claudia said. "I hope not."

Their smiling, bald-headed waiter appeared and Steve ordered two glasses of champagne. They perused the menu and discussed the options.

"I'd like to order duck," Claudia said. "But after seeing those darling ducks floating along in the stream outside, I can't. Even though that's what I feed Wrigley—duck and green pea cat food. Now I feel guilty."

Steve chuckled. "You're adorable. They have some vegetarian dishes."

When their waiter reappeared with two glasses of champagne, they ordered the Moroccan Stew made of chickpeas and vegetables.

Steve raised his glass. "To us. We're a great team."

She grinned and clinked glasses.

After they'd both taken a sip, Steve said, "You know, I still think Wrigley was on the right track about marriage. A lot of young people nowadays think marriage is an antiquated idea."

Claudia slumped in her seat. "This again?"

"I think we should make some determination as to where we're headed," Steve said, matter-of-factly.

"Aren't we doing fine as we are?"

"Exactly." Steve sounded quite sure of himself. "Half of marriages end in divorce. A marriage license is just a piece of paper, after all."

Claudia found herself taking umbrage. "Well, that's a dumb old argument. I thought a police detective would have more respect for the law. A license is a legal document, isn't it? It makes a relationship lawful, so if you were in a hospital, I'd be able to visit you."

Steve shrugged. "But we're both healthy."

"Peter died in a hospital. If I wasn't married to him, I wouldn't have been allowed to be with him at the end."

Steve nodded in a serious way. "You have a point there. Any other arguments to make?"

"Married people get tax breaks."

"That's not a very romantic reason," Steve said.

"This whole conversation isn't very romantic," Claudia replied. "We're supposed to be celebrating, not arguing. Can't we talk about something else?"

"Okay." He leaned back in his chair. "What should we talk about?"

"What happened when you booked Stanislaus?"

"He gave us a full confession. Bawled his eyes out. I believe he really didn't intend to kill Mrs. Worthington. He'd left a basement window unlocked when he was cleaning. It's at the side of the house. The security system was off."

"Is that how he got in when he tried to steal Wrigley?"

"Yup. And he snuck in the same way today, shortly before we got there. He was in the living room when he heard us unlocking the door, so he ducked behind the screen. And luckily you saw him." Steve raised his glass to her.

After they sipped champagne, Steve asked how things were going at the cat clinic. Claudia told him they'd had an increase of new clients since they'd been in the news as the place Wrigley was taken.

Their plates of Moroccan Stew were brought and they ate in silence for a while, which made Claudia nervous. Steve seemed to be preoccupied in his own thoughts. They ordered desserts, apple pie ala mode for him and key lime pie for her. While they were waiting, Steve leaned forward.

"I've been thinking, another reason not to marry is we won't have to hassle about which house we'll live in, yours or mine. Staying single allows us to remain independent, something you seem to enjoy."

Claudia sighed. "I suppose," she agreed in a dreary tone.

"Don't you like being independent? I keep getting that impression."

"It has its perks. But having someone to come home to is nice."

"Being single, you're free to make your own decisions," he argued.

"Two heads are better than one," she retorted. *Why am I coming up with that old saw?*

"But not everyone is suited being a cop's spouse. We work long hours sometimes."

She shifted in her seat and looked at him in a troubled way. "I think I've adjusted pretty well to your work."

"You worry about me a lot," he pointed out.

"Yes, but I've seen how well-trained you are. You know how to handle yourself. You have good people as back-up. And you're right, Briarwood is a pretty safe town. I guess I shouldn't worry so much."

"Okay. All right." He nodded with finality. "You've convinced me." He started searching his jacket pocket. "Therefore . . . ."

Pulling out a small box, he set it on the white tablecloth.

Claudia stared at the rounded, velvet-covered object. "What's . . . that?"

Steve opened the box and all at once she found herself staring dumbfounded at a solitaire diamond ring, luminous and sparkling in the restaurant's ceiling lights. She clasped her hands to her face as tears started in her eyes. Laughing and crying at the same time, she said, "Why were you arguing against . . . ? You tricked me!"

"I hoped a little reverse psychology might help me plead my case," he admitted. "Wrigley made me think of it. You know I fell in love with you the first time I met you, when you were wearing that outfit with cartoon cats all over it. I didn't think I'd ever love again. But suddenly, there you were."

She blotted away tears with her napkin. Then she noticed that people at the tables nearby were watching them with eager interest.

"Everyone's waiting for your answer," Steve said. "Time to make a decision."

Claudia drew in a deep breath before speaking. "I'm sorry I've been avoiding your hints. To tell you the truth, even though I do love you, the idea of marriage unsettles me. Even scares me a little. I've adjusted so well to being single, I'm not sure I can re-adjust to sharing my life with someone again." She gazed into his troubled eyes. A new tear slid down her cheek. She quickly wiped it away. "But I don't want to take the risk of losing you, so . . . yes, Steve, I'll marry you."

His face broke into a huge smile. "We'll figure out our future together." He took the ring from the box and held out his hand. She obligingly placed her left hand in his, feeling breathless at the life-altering step she was taking. As he slipped the ring on her finger, people at nearby tables applauded.

Claudia gazed at the ring gleaming on her hand. "It's beautiful," she murmured. And she found herself growing calm, now that she'd finally made a decision. She looked into Steve's adoring eyes. "We do make a good team. Hope you won't mind living with three cats."

"Wrigley's already my buddy. He gave me the clue to how to persuade you."

Their waiter brought their desserts just then. "I see congratulations are in order," he said, eyeing her ring. "I'll be right back." In a few minutes he returned with two new glasses of champagne. "On the house."

Steve raised his glass. "To my charming cat collector and wife-to-be."

"To the longsuffering detective who never gave up on me."

They clinked glasses and took a sip. Claudia hesitated digging into her key lime pie, still feeling choked up with emotion.

"Claudia!"

She turned to find Amy approaching their table. "Hi, Amy."

"I didn't know you were here," Amy said with enthusiasm. "Steve, how are you?"

"Great," he replied.

"We sat on the other side of the restaurant," Amy explained. "Larry's getting the car. Word went from table to table that some guy proposed to his girlfriend here. So, you know me, I had to snoop around a little to see."

Claudia began laughing and held up her left hand, wiggling her fingers to make the solitaire sparkle.

"Oh, my gosh, it's you?!" Amy glanced back and forth at the two of them. "Way to go, Steve! You broke down her defenses. I've been rooting for you."

Steve stood and gave Amy a hug. "Thanks. I needed all the support I could get."

211

As Steve sat down again, Amy looked at Claudia, eyes aglow. "What fun it'll be to plan your wedding!"

As usual, Amy was moving too fast for Claudia's comfort, but she rose and gave Amy a warm embrace. "I'm sure I'll need some help."

"Well, gotta go," Amy said, as Claudia took her seat again. "Congratulations, you guys!"

When Amy was out of earshot, Claudia gazed at Steve with a happy sort of exasperation. "Heaven knows what kind of wedding we're in for."

Steve reached across the table, took her hands in his and said, "Any style of wedding is fine with me, as long as you're my bride and I'm your groom."

"Amen to that."

RECIPE

Author's Note: I try to cook a vegetarian meal once a week. I mentioned this dish in my story because it's a favorite of mine. Here's the recipe for the "Moroccan Stew" Claudia and Steve ordered at The Old Mill.

Moroccan Potato, Carrot, and Chickpea Stew

Serves 4; 30 minutes or fewer

2 Tbs. olive oil
1 large russet potato (12 oz.) cut into ¾ inch cubes
8 oz. peeled baby carrots (1 ¾ cups)
2 Large shallots, diced (1 cup) (onion works well, too)
½ tsp. salt
½ tsp. ground black pepper
1 15.5 oz. can low-sodium chickpeas, drained with liquid reserved, divided
1/3 cup dark raisins
1 ¼ tsp. ground cumin
½ tsp. pumpkin pie spice
2 Tbs. lemon juice
4 oz. fresh spinach leaves (2 cups)

Directions:

1. Heat oil in large skillet over medium-high heat. Add potato, carrots, shallots, salt and pepper; sauté 3 minutes.
2. Add chickpea liquid, raisins, cumin, and pumpkin pie spice. Toss to blend, and bring to a simmer.
3. Cover; simmer over medium-low heat 8 minutes. Mix in 1 cup chickpeas. Cover and simmer 2 to 4 minutes more, or until potato and carrots are just tender.
4. Place remaining chickpeas on a plate and mash coarsely with a fork.
5. Mix crushed chickpeas and lemon juice into stew.
6. Mound spinach on top. Toss gently 1 to 2 minutes, or until spinach is reduced in volume, adding more water, salt and pepper if desired.

Per 1 cup serving: 343 cal; 11 g protein; 8 g total fat (1 g sat fat); 60 g carb; 0 mg chol; 381 mg sodium; 8 g fiber; 15 g sugars (from Vegetarian Times Magazine)

ABOUT THE AUTHOR

Lori Herter grew up in the suburbs of Chicago, graduated from the University of Illinois, Chicago Campus, and worked for several years at the Chicago Association of Commerce & Industry. She married her husband, Jerry, a CPA, and they moved to Southern California a few decades ago. They still live there and have been "mom and dad" to a number of cats over the years. Currently, they are down to one cat, Jazzy, a Himalayan who does not appreciate other felines in the household.

Lori and Jerry have traveled extensively in the U.S., Canada, Europe, New Zealand and Australia, and Tahiti. Lori's favorite destination of all is Ireland. A pet sitter whom Jazzy likes almost as much as us takes care of her while we are away.

Lori has written romance novels published by Dell Candlelight Romances, Silhouette, and Harlequin. Some of these books are currently available as ebooks on Amazon and Barnes & Noble. She also wrote a four-book romantic vampire series, one of the first of the genre, published by Berkley with the titles OBSESSION, POSSESSION, CONFESSION, and ETERNITY. Her vampire novella "Cimarron Spirit" is included in the New York Times best-selling anthology, EDGE OF DARKNESS published by Berkley. Two individually published sequels by Lori,

CIMARRON SECRETS and CIMARRON SEDUCTRESS, are available on Amazon. Her book set in Ireland featuring Irish fairy lore, THE THIN PLACE, is also available on Amazon.

Lori's website is <u>www.loriherter.com</u>